Mail Order Matchup
Book 46 in Brides of Beckham
Kirsten Osbourne

Chapter One

Florence sat in the parlor under the watchful eye of her mother, waiting for her fiancé Arthur Pratt to arrive. They were to discuss the final guest list for their wedding which was set for three months away. She and her mother had worked hard to pare down the list to just fifty people she would invite, and Arthur was supposed to have done the same with his list.

There was a knock at the door, and Florence smiled at her mother. "May we have just one minute of privacy?" she asked.

Her mother shook her head as she always did. "After you're married."

Florence sighed. "You're so old-fashioned. Some of my friends get five whole minutes with no chaperone!"

"You'll thank me for being old fashioned when you have daughters of your own."

Florence wasn't so certain. As soon as Arthur walked into the room, she smiled, simply feeling her entire being light up at the presence of the man she loved so dearly. "Arthur! Good evening!"

There was no smile on his face as he nodded first to her mother and then Florence. He took his normal spot beside Florence on the sofa, but he didn't sit as close as usual. It was as if he was avoiding her touch.

Florence smiled at him tentatively. "Do you have your guest list?" she asked, noting that his hands were empty. Of course, he could have put the list into his pocket.

He shook his head. "I need to tell you something, Florence." He looked down at his hands, which were twisting on his lap. "I can't marry you."

Florence heard her mother gasp, even as she felt the shock run through her body. "Why not?"

"I'm afraid while you and your parents spent the month at sea in June, I stepped out with Alice Humphreys."

Florence shook her head. "No, Arthur. You wouldn't do that."

"But I did. And she's expecting. I married her this afternoon."

She stared at him for a moment, then did the first thing that came to her mind. She hit him over the head with the papers in her hand with all her might. Realizing that probably didn't hurt him enough, she stood up, gave him a swift kick in the shin, and then slapped his face.

"Go. I never want to look at you again, Arthur Pratt!"

He stood. "I'm so sorry, Florence. I still love you, but I can't shirk my duty."

She kicked him once more for good measure. "You are a bounder and a cad. I never want to see you again. Do you hear me?"

Arthur didn't have to be told a third time. He rushed out of the room, and they heard the front door close behind them. Florence would have thought she would feel sad if her entire life plans had been ruined in a moment, but she didn't. Instead, she was angry. She was so angry that she wanted to spit, but polite young ladies didn't.

Florence sat back down on her normal spot on the sofa and ripped her guest list in half. "Well, that wasn't what I expected to happen," she finally said while her mother sat staring at her with her mouth agape.

"I have never seen you act that way toward anyone, Florence." Her mother shook her head. "Why would you kick him?"

"He just ruined my entire life, Mother. I've been planning to marry him since I was fifteen, and now that we're finally old enough to marry, he's cheated on me and has to marry another? I will not forgive him for this."

"Boys talk," her mother said. "Do you honestly think you'll find another man to marry after you kicked him and slapped him? Truly?"

"Does it matter?" Florence asked. "I'll be the laughingstock of the whole town anyway! Send me to stay with grandmother while the talk dies down. I beg of you!"

"Your grandmother is in Europe this month. It would make no sense at all for you to go to her. No, you'll have to stay here and keep your chin up."

"Fine! Then I'll go to Mrs. Tandy and tell her I want to be a mail-order bride. She'll send me away if you won't."

To Florence's dismay, her mother laughed. "You would never be able to handle the life of a mail-order bride. Those women are required to cook, clean, and mind children."

Florence didn't know what possessed her, but her mother's laughter, added more fuel to the fire that was burning inside her. Instead of being laughed at more, Florence walked to the front door and left. Never had she gone anywhere without a maid as chaperone, but she was going to today.

She walked the three houses down to the Tandy residence and knocked on the door, not even able to smile when Mr. Tandy came to the door. "I need to see Mrs. Tandy please."

"Yes, of course, Miss Florence. She's in her study. It's the last door on the left."

Florence didn't wait to be shown to Mrs. Tandy's office. Instead, she strode through the house as if she owned it and opened the door without knocking.

Elizabeth Tandy looked up, obviously surprised. "Miss Ashton."

Florence nodded once, walking into the room and taking a seat on the sofa opposite Mrs. Tandy's desk. "I want to be a mail-order bride, and if you can make it happen, I want to leave yesterday."

"But...I thought you were to marry Arthur Pratt."

"I was, but he stepped out on me and got Alice Humphreys pregnant. So before the gossip spreads all over town, I want to leave and marry someone who doesn't have loose morals."

Mrs. Tandy smiled and nodded. "Let me see who I have here." She picked up a stack of papers, and finally smiled. "This one.

Florence took the letter and read it quickly.

Dear Matchmaker,

My name is Jacob Weatherby, and I'm a banker in Cheyenne, Wyoming. My parents died when I was just fifteen, and my twin brother, and only other living relative, died five years ago. I'm rather alone in the world and want to change that.

Do not worry about cooking or housekeeping skills, as I have a housekeeper who cares for those things. What I need is a woman I can fall in love with. Not too thin and not too fat. I'd like her to be between the ages of eighteen and twenty-four, and I would prefer she never married.

I have no children, and more than anything need a companion. I have many business suppers, and I need a wife to plan the supper and make sure everything is just so. For this, I would prefer a wife who was raised with wealth, but if someone can be taught, that will be just as good.

Having a wife here quickly is imperative. Please send me a telegram as to the date and time of her arrival, and I will be at the train depot, waiting for her.

Thank you for working with me in this matter.

Sincerely,

Jacob Weatherby

Florence handed the letter back to Mrs. Tandy. "He'll do. When do I leave?"

Mrs. Tandy blinked a couple of times. "How quickly can you pack all your belongings?"

"I'll stay up all night and get it done tonight. It's not like I have a great many things to do without a wedding to plan."

"I should be able to get you on the ten a.m. train then. Will that suit you?"

"It will. Please send someone to collect me at nine-thirty. I will have all of my belongings ready to go."

The utter shock on Mrs. Tandy's face surprised Florence. "Is it unusual for someone to agree to marry so quickly?" she asked.

"It's unusual for a daughter of wealthy parents to come see me at all. It's happened a few times, but no one has shown quite the spirit you have." Elizabeth smiled. "Would you like some cookies before you go?"

Florence shook her head. "No, but thank you. I have had supper. I'll see you or whomever you send bright and early tomorrow morning. Good evening." Florence headed for the front door, needing to be away from people who gave her a look of sympathy. She needed to take care of business, and she didn't need anyone around her while she did it.

Instead of heading straight home, Florence walked around the block once before going to speak with her parents. Her mother remained where Florence had left her in the parlor, and her father joined her.

She went straight into the parlor, knowing she had to tell her parents about her decision and knowing they wouldn't be happy with her. That was all right, though, because she wasn't happy with anyone or anything then. They could all be miserable together.

She walked in and sat in an empty chair, looking between her parents. "I talked to Mrs. Tandy, and she is sending me to marry a man in Cheyenne, Wyoming. He's a banker there. I'll be leaving in the morning, and plan to spend the night packing, and then I will hopefully sleep on the train tomorrow."

Her father nodded. "I think that's a good choice. You're embroiled in a scandal, and I want it touching the three of us as little as possible."

Her mother shook her head. "But you don't know how to cook!"

"He has a housekeeper. I won't be cooking. I won't be cleaning. I'll be planning parties and being a good hostess, just as I would have done if I'd married Arthur. The man's name is Jacob Weatherby."

Her father nodded. "All right." He looked at her mother. "Susan, I would appreciate it if you spent as much time as you could tonight helping our daughter pack for her trip to Cheyenne."

"But...she can't just marry a stranger. She's been raised to be pampered and loved, not to work herself to death." Her mother looked truly fearful for her daughter.

"He's expecting a young lady raised in wealth," Florence said. "I'm certain I'll fill his needs beautifully. Now I'm going upstairs to pack my belongings." Thankfully, her trousseau was already finished and packed into three large trunks. She would be able to get the rest of her belongings into another two or three. It would be work, but it wouldn't be nearly as hard as it could have been. Putting words to her actions, she stood and went upstairs. She didn't care what her parents thought of what she was doing. It was her life, and she was going to live it to the fullest.

Upstairs, she opened another of the trunks her parents had bought for her to pack all of her belongings into for the move to Arthur's place. Even though she wasn't packing as she'd planned to pack, she was doing what she needed to do. She'd be Jacob's wife in a week, and she looked forward to the opportunity to show off her skills in party planning.

Before her mother joined her, she had finished packing up the first trunk and was working on the second. She had more clothes than she'd realized, and she ran her hand down the front of her wedding gown before carefully packing it in tissue paper and putting it at the bottom of her trunk.

She had few personal things she cared to take with her, mostly consisting of childhood memories. There was a china doll whose eyes opened and closed, dressed in a pink silk dress, a handful of her favorite books, and a small jewelry box filled with all of the jewelry she had collected over the years.

Most of what she had to take with her were clothes. Thankfully, she had all new clothes as she'd gotten ready for her wedding. Nothing would be needed before her trip.

When her mother came into her room, it was mostly bare. Only the sheets and pillows were left on the bed, and she planned to take one of the pillows for the train. Her mother sat on the side of her bed. "Your father asked me to give you this," Mother said softly. "It's extra money, so you can get a sleeping car on the train if your affianced doesn't get one for you. And there's money for food along the way and even enough for return fare if he is cruel."

Florence accepted the money with a nod. "Thank you, Mother."

"I want you to be happy," her mother said softly.

"I plan to make the most of the situation in Cheyenne. I'll be a good wife to him, and he should be a good husband to me. I'll find some charity work to do and stay busy, as you've taught me." Florence had never been particularly close to her mother, but she had learned from her and always did as she was told.

"I hope you'll write to me as soon as you arrive," Mother said softly. "I need to know that you're happy and comfortable. I worry the man you plan to marry is cruel or something."

"I'm not worried even a little bit, Mother. I'll do just fine. If he's cruel, I'll leave. I refuse to stay with a man who steps out on me or mistreats me."

"Men step out on their wives," Mother said. "You'll need to understand that and accept it as face. Especially if a man has money, he will have a mistress."

Florence raised an eyebrow. "If you want to live that way, then you may, but I will not. I have too much self-respect for that."

"Then you'll spend the rest of your life alone," Mother predicted. "I've done my best to raise you with an understanding of how the world works. I pray that you'll do the right thing and turn a blind eye when your husband is the one stepping out."

Florence shook her head. "No, I won't. But thank you for the advice, Mother."

When her mother left, Florence's mind was spinning. Had her father cheated on her mother? Was that why the woman was so cold and unfeeling? She had no idea, but she truly hoped her mother would understand that she couldn't follow in her footsteps and do such a thing.

It was after midnight when Florence had finished everything she'd planned to do that night. She tucked a small sum of the money her mother had given to her into each of her trunks, and some into her reticule. Some would go into her cleavage and other money into her shoes. Perhaps her mother would never approve, but she would not arrive in Cheyenne penniless.

As soon as she finished, she collapsed into her bed, realizing this was the last time she would sleep in her childhood bedroom and the last time she would sleep under her father's roof. Her life would change dramatically the next day as she left Beckham, but it would change for the better. And if it didn't, she would change her circumstances until it was better.

Chapter Two

Jacob stood on the platform in Cheyenne waiting for the train. He looked at his pocket watch for the third time just as a train pulled in. His gaze scanned the crowd as people got off the train, but Florence was unmistakable. She was the only lady of truly refined tastes to get off the train in a beautiful lavender dress and matching parasol.

He walked over and smiled at her. "Florence?" The woman was beautiful, and he stared at her for perhaps longer than he should have.

She nodded. "Yes, you must be Jacob."

"My friends and family call me Jake," he said.

"I thought you had no family?" Florence looked at him curiously.

"No, I guess I don't. I've always been called Jake. We'll leave it at that." He offered her his arm. "You have luggage?" he asked.

"Yes, six trunks. I see one of them on the platform now."

He nodded to a man who was not far behind him. "Six trunks. Miss Florence Ashton." Then he began walking. "Do you need something to eat, or should we go straight to the church?"

"I must admit I'm hungry, but I'm not sure anything would stay down because I'm more nervous than hungry," she said.

"Then let's go to the church and have Pastor Ryan marry us."

She nodded regally, surprised she wasn't feeling like running away from him and screaming. He seemed to be a good man, at least so far. But she'd once thought Arthur was a good man.

"I'm surprised a lady like yourself isn't already married?"

"I was supposed to have a wedding. I was in the middle of planning it when my fiancé told me he'd gotten another young lady in the family way and had married her. My mother tried to convince me that's just what men do, but I won't have it. I want your promise to never stray."

She hadn't meant to bring up the subject so quickly, but now that she had, she wouldn't marry him without the promise.

"I promise. And now I expect the same promise from you."

She smiled, just a tilt of her lips. "I promise as well."

"I'm glad that's out of the way," he said, wiping fake sweat off his brow.

"As am I," she said, not joking at all. "How far is the church?"

He pointed to a building just ahead. "Right there. It's our church and school."

"I see. Wonderful. We'll marry, and then I'll beg you to feed me."

"You won't still worry about the food coming back up if we're already married when you eat?"

"That's right. Until we speak our vows, there's always the chance you'll tell me you're already married or something of the sort. I have no desire to be married to a man who is already married or who is in a physical relationship with another woman."

"You'll be happy to know I'm neither of those things," he said, opening the door to the church and waiting as she walked through.

Once they reached the front of the church, a pastor was there to lead them through the ceremony. "I brought my wife and her sister as your two witnesses," the pastor said.

Florence nodded. "Thank you, pastor."

Within minutes they were married, and he was bestowing a chaste kiss on her lips. After paying the pastor for the service, Jake led her out of the church and down the street to a restaurant.

Florence had eaten in restaurants, of course, but none that were quite that...rowdy was the only word she could come up with. There were men in denim trousers and cowboy hats all over the establishment. She wasn't certain if she should be frightened or fascinated, so she chose fascination.

"Are there a great many men who dress that way here?" she asked.

He laughed. "A lot more than wear suits, I'm afraid." He himself was wearing a three-piece black suit with a bow tie. Perfect for a banker.

"That's not how people dress back east," she said, looking all around here, trying to memorize what she was seeing so she could write home. Her best friend, MaryJane, didn't even know she was leaving, so she would need a letter quickly.

"No, but it's a different world out here. Our economy is based on ranching, and men dress for their work."

"I'm certain, I'll get used to it soon."

"I'm certain you will too." He picked up his menu and read over the offerings as she did the same. "What do you want to have?" he asked.

"I believe I'll have a hamburger. I've read about them and always wanted to try one, but my mother said they weren't ladylike. Would you mind?"

He shook his head, trying to hide his amusement. He was fond of hamburgers himself. "I'll have one too. They come with fried potatoes."

"Sounds delicious," she said. Of course, she'd never had fried potatoes, but she'd watch how he ate his, and she would do just fine.

He gave the waiter their order, and he said he'd be back in a moment with water. "We'll have two Coca-Colas as well," Jake said.

"I've read about Coca-Cola as well. Is it as good as advertised?"

"I think so, and you're about to find out for yourself," he said, smiling. "I'm glad you're willing to try new things."

"Oh, I certainly am. My mother kept a very tight rein on me, expecting me to be perfect in all things. I figure if I'm going to live somewhere like Cheyenne, I need to learn to eat the local cuisine."

"I find most things palatable. My mother was very experimental with her cooking, and I've never found a cook who can hold a candle to her." He sighed as he thought about his mostly idyllic childhood.

"How did your parents die?" he asked.

"Mother was filling in for a teller at the bank when it was robbed. She and Father were both killed in the ensuing gunfire."

She reached for his hand covering it with her own. "I'm so sorry. I cannot imagine losing either of my parents."

"Thank you," he said softly. "Thankfully, we had servants who finished bringing us up, and made sure we trained for work at the bank."

"Did your father work at the bank?" she asked.

"My parents owned the bank," he told her. "And then my brother and I owned the bank. And now I own the bank."

"What happened to your brother?"

"Jesse? He was out taking a walk, and a hunter's bullet hit him by mistake."

"It sounds like you've had more than your share of misfortunes," she said. "I truly hope the rest of your life is better than the life you've had so far."

"I hope so too. But how could it not be better, considering it is starting by marrying you?" he asked, a smile on his face.

"You're very sweet," she responded. *And handsome.*

"Well, thank you. After lunch, I'll take you home, show you around, and then I have a meeting at the bank at four. I'm sorry I couldn't cancel it, but it's a very important meeting."

"That's all right. I understand that men have busy work schedules, and it's a woman's job to make her husband's life easier not harder. Complaining about your work hours would only make your life harder."

"I'm glad that's your attitude." Their burgers arrived then, and he showed her how to pick up the burger by holding the bread on either side of the meat. Then he put it to his mouth and bit right off of it, not even cutting a bite off.

She copied his movements, carefully holding the burger so as to not lose anything off the bread, and she took a big bite of it. She chewed slowly and smiled. "Oh, that's delicious."

"I think so too," he said, wiping his mouth with a napkin. Then he picked up one of the pieces of fried potato, cut into long strings, and popped it into his mouth. "You're going to love the potatoes too."

He watched as she did she same as he had, picking up the potato and putting it into her mouth and chewing it thoroughly. "Oh, that's delicious too!"

He grinned. "I'm glad you think so. It's one of my favorite things to eat, though my housekeeper refuses to make hamburgers and fries. She says they're for the lower class, and I shouldn't be eating them."

"So we'll have to sneak here to get them. Easy enough," she said, winking at him.

He laughed, loving her playful nature. This was a woman he could spend the rest of his life with and never even think about straying. She had spirit, and that's what he'd been looking for in a wife.

After paying their bill, he offered her his arm, and they left the restaurant to walk through the busy streets of Cheyenne. He pointed out a few places she may wish to go along the way, including a store that was just for clothing. She'd never imagined such a thing. She almost wished she hadn't brought so much clothing with her so she could shop at the store.

He led her through the streets, which all seemed to be filled with men who either owned or worked cattle, to the largest house within seeing distance. He opened the door and smiled, happy to finally be bringing a bride home to the house he'd grown up in.

He led through a dining room with beautiful mahogany furniture to the kitchen, where an older woman was cooking something. "Mrs. Andrews, I'd like you to meet my wife, Florence. Florence, Mrs. Andrews raised me as her own after my parents died."

"It's so nice to meet you, Mrs. Andrews," Florence said, smiling and nodding at the woman.

"And you, Mrs. Weatherby. I do hope we'll become friends."

"I hope so as well. I am glad there's someone else to cook around here. I've done little cooking myself, and I'm afraid I'd be lost if left in a kitchen alone."

Mrs. Andrews smiled. "Cooking is my job. If you ever want something special, you just let me know."

Feeling mischievous, Florence said, "I'd really love a hamburger and potato fries. Could you make those sometime soon?"

"I'd be happy to," Mrs. Andrews said. "As soon as hell freezes over."

Florence giggled at the other woman's response. "Jake told me how you feel about cooking those things, so I just had to tease."

"I can see we're going to get along very well," Mrs. Andrews said to Florence. "I'm making chicken, mashed potatoes, gravy, and broccoli for supper. Does that suit you, ma'am?"

"It suits me beautifully," Florence said. "Thank you."

Jake hadn't been able to stop grinning since he and Florence had stepped into the kitchen. The woman may have been a stranger just a couple of hours before, but she was going to be the best wife he could have possibly asked for. He could feel it in his bones.

"Let's leave Mrs. Andrews to her cooking, and I'll show you the rest of the house."

He took her through four parlors, one a musical parlor, one filled with beautiful art, and one simply called the blue parlor. "I usually use the front parlor for every day and the blue parlor for guests," he said.

"That works for me." She looked up the long staircase. "Is there a bathroom?"

"Two, actually," he said. "One downstairs and one up. Come, I'll show you."

Florence was relieved. She'd gotten so used to having an indoor bathroom, she wasn't certain she could adjust to an outhouse. After showing her the downstairs bath, he led her up the stairs to the upstairs bath, and then he opened a door wide.

Inside was a huge bed as well as a dresser and an armoire. "I'm not sure all your clothes are going to fit," he said. "We may need another armoire."

"We may," she said, refusing to apologize for her clothing. Why should she?

He grinned. "I had Albert put all your trunks on the other side of the bed. If you need help unpacking, I'm certain Mrs. Andrews would be happy to help."

"Thank you," she said. "The room is beautiful."

"That bed is going to look a lot better to me with you in it," he said, winking at her.

"Well, I'll certainly get into it at the first opportunity then. Even with a sleeping car on the train, I'm afraid I didn't sleep well."

He frowned. "You should nap while I'm at the bank this afternoon them. There's nothing else you need to do."

"Except unpack six trunks," she said with a smile. "But I may take you up on that nap first. Please tell me we're not entertaining guests tonight."

"Oh, no. Not until next week."

"Good. That will give us time to get used to each other's habits first." Florence was most excited about getting used to him in bed. She knew it wasn't something a proper young lady thought about, but she wasn't a proper young lady either. She was simply Florence.

He smiled and nodded. "That's what I was thinking." He eyed her curiously for a moment and then asked what he'd wanted to ask since the church. "May I kiss you again? A real kiss this time?"

"I'd like that," she told him, tilting her head up to look into his deep brown eyes.

He lowered his head and lightly brushed his lips against hers, but then deepened the kiss. He tilted his head to the side and his tongue traced her lips. She gasped when she realized when he was doing, and he took that as an invitation to explore her mouth more deeply.

When he lifted his head five minutes later, she was out of breath, and he was out of focus. For a moment she wondered what had just happened to her, as she felt something aching deep inside her. She stood looking up at his blurred face for a moment, but then she went back into his arms, this time initiating the kiss herself.

Finally, when he released her once more, he shook his head. "You pack a wallop, Mrs. Weatherby."

"As do you," she said softly, wishing they had time to make use of the bed right then.

"I have to go to the bank, but I'll be home soon. And after dinner, we're coming up here, and I'm having my way with you."

"Are you sure I won't be having my way with you?" she asked, feeling daring.

He chuckled. "We'll have our way with each other, and we'll both enjoy it immensely."

"Is that so?"

"It is. I've decided." He kissed her forehead. "Get that nap. I want you alert tonight."

With that, he left the room, and she watched him go, clinging to one of his bedposts. How did she already feel so much more for Jake than she'd ever felt for Arthur?

Chapter Three

Florence took the opportunity to nap while Jake was gone, but first she dug through her trunks until she found the one with the nightclothes she'd had made for her honeymoon. When she found the gown she'd planned to wear for her wedding night, she laid it on top of everything in the trunk, and then closed the lid so Jacke wouldn't see it.

She wanted to make him swallow his tongue on their wedding night, which was happening just as she'd wanted it to. It was Thursday, so they would soon have the weekend to look forward to.

She crawled between the sheets of his bed, fully clothed, needing sleep more than she needed anything else the world had to offer. When she closed her eyes, her body took her back to the kisses she'd shared with Jake a short while before. She wasn't sure what it was, but his kisses had her feeling more than Arthur's ever had. Hopefully, she'd married the right man. At that moment, it certainly felt like it.

She woke to Jake entering their bedroom, moving silently. He'd kicked off his shoes, but she still heard his walk through the sleep hazed world. "Is everything all right?" she asked, feeling guilty about him catching her in a nap, but she'd needed the sleep badly enough that she pushed the guilt away.

"Yes, it's just time for supper, so I thought I should wake you."

"Did I really sleep for that long?" she asked.

"You were tired," was his only response. He offered her a hand to help her from the bed. He wasn't certain if he was supposed to or not, but if he offered a lady a hand when she was standing from a seated position, it only made sense to him that he did the same from lying down. "Are you hungry?"

To her surprise, she was. She took his hand and got out of the bed, a little embarrassed when her skirt rode up higher than was acceptable, but then she remembered this man was her husband, and he would be seeing a great deal more in just a few hours. "How was your meeting?" she asked, putting her clothing to rights.

"It was good. Now I don't have to work until Monday."

"You don't work Fridays?" she asked, surprised.

"I don't work the day after I marry. I felt bad enough going in for an hour today, but it was necessary. The young lady who I met with needed funds immediately."

For a moment, Florence worried about him meeting with a young lady, but she told herself he could have married the other woman if that had been his inclination. "I'm glad you met with her then," she said, not letting jealousy color her voice. There was no reason for her to be jealous. He'd married her, hadn't he?

Noticing he wasn't wearing his shoes, she decided to go down to supper barefoot as well. Her mother would have been disgusted with her, but it felt good to be barefoot sometimes.

"I can't wait to try Mrs. Andrews's cooking. Our cook back home was very fussy, and he only fixed dishes he considered high class enough for the family. I do hope Mrs. Andrews isn't that way."

"The only thing I've not been able to talk her into making are hamburgers, but we can go out when we want those."

Florence grinned at Jake. "I like the way you think."

Jake smiled, pleased that they understood one another as well as they did. "Her chicken is wonderful, and you'll be treated to that tonight."

"I'm excited. I feel like my culinary experience is going to be widened, and who could complain about that?"

When they got to the dining room, there was a place setting at each end of the long table. It felt ridiculous to her, so she picked up her place setting and moved it at a right angle to his. "There. I don't think we should need to shout down the table at one another."

"I agree. My parents did that, and it always made me wonder why they didn't like one another? It was so odd to me."

"My parents were the same. I don't want to be that way, though." She was certain part of why her mother was so distant was her belief that men always had mistresses. She wasn't going to have that kind of marriage, and if her husband needed warmth and affection, he should seek her out, not a stranger.

Mrs. Andrews seemed a bit surprised at the rearrangement of places, though she said nothing. She placed the meal on the table, and they were to serve themselves, which Florence liked better than how the cook had done things back home. If she wanted a little more mashed potatoes, and a little less chicken, that should be up to her and not the cook.

Once their places were fixed, Jake took her hand in his and said a quick prayer, thanking God for their food and delivering her safely from Massachusetts.

When Florence took her first bite of the mashed potatoes, she closed her eyes and let the flavors dance through her mouth. "This is the best gravy I've ever tasted in my life. It's fabulous!"

Jake grinned. "Wait til you try the chicken."

Florence carefully cut a piece from the fried chicken and popped it into her mouth. Only after it was swallowed did she say, "You're right. The chicken is even better. I should have her teach me to cook!"

"Why?" he asked. "You won't have an opportunity to use the skill, so it makes more sense to spend your time doing other things."

"I guess you're right. But I would love to be able to cook a meal and see you enjoy it as much as I'm enjoying this one."

"I go to a lake house every year for a month in the summer. I take Mrs. Andrews with me so I don't miss out on her cooking."

"What if she was called away because of a death in the family?"

"Her daughter would take her place," he said. "She's done it before, and her cooking is almost as good as her mother's."

She sighed. "Foiled before I even had my first lesson."

He chuckled. "Your job is to be a good wife, to plan parties, and to look pretty. What else could I ask of you?"

"I'll that as a compliment. I certainly hope my party planning skills are as good as you're expecting. The biggest party I ever planned was my wedding, and that never took place."

"I know you'll do just fine," he said. "There's just something about you that screams competence. I know you'll do anything you set your mind to."

She smiled sweetly, inwardly praying she would be able to do as he said and plan perfect parties. "I'll do my very best, no matter what the circumstances," she said softly.

"Oh, good, because we're hosting a small supper on Tuesday night. We'll have five couples as our guests. And I need you to plan everything."

"All right. I'll consult with Mrs. Andrews about the meal we'd like to serve tomorrow. Supper at six?" she asked.

"Yes, supper at six. Most will be gone by nine. Hopefully earlier. I just want you to get to know some of the prominent women in the community. I invited two ranchers and their wives, a merchant and his wife, a local railroad man and his wife, and the mayor and his wife. It should prove to be an excellent introduction to the society of Cheyenne."

"That sounds wonderful," she said, not sure that she meant it. Most society women she'd met could be rather catty, and she certainly didn't need that kind of negativity.

After they'd finished their meal, Mrs. Andrews came in with a cake, complete with delicate flowers made from the white frosting. "Every couple needs a wedding cake, and I don't care if they were married privately." She cut two large slices of cake and put them on small plates.

Looking at the cake, Florence was reminded of the huge cake she'd chosen to be made for her own wedding. She hoped the merchants she'd dealt with weren't thinking negatively of her for having to cancel the way she did.

As she popped the first bite of cake into her mouth, Florence sighed. "I'm going to get fat living here. I do hope you will still find me attractive."

"I want you to get fat with our children, and yes, I will find that very attractive."

"How many children would you like?" she asked.

"Well, there was only my brother and me, and now that he's gone I'm alone. So I'd like at least six. Every child should have siblings to play with and make mischief with."

She nodded. "You're not alone anymore," she said covering his hand with hers, "and I agree about siblings. I was an only child, and I hated it. I had one friend my mother approved of, and we've remained close, but she had many siblings of her own. I felt as if I was missing out."

"Good. Then we're agreed on a dozen...err...six children!"

Laughing softly, she said, "I'd be happy with a dozen as well. I want a house full of children."

"I do too." He lowered his voice. "I look forward to making them."

She blushed but nodded. "I do too."

He chuckled. "You're supposed to be all embarrassed that I said that and tell me to hush. Aren't you?"

She shrugged. "I have no idea, honestly. My mother went over the etiquette of dinner parties, and weddings, and receptions, and christenings. She never said a word about how a wife should react to a teasing advance from her husband."

"Well, then I guess we're forging our own road, aren't we?" He loved that her reactions were so real. There was nothing fake about her, and that's exactly what he wanted in a wife. She was perfect for him.

After supper, they went to the parlor, and for the first time, she noticed all the books in the room. "Do you have a library?" she asked.

"I do. These are the books I was too lazy to return to their proper place after finishing them."

"I want to see the library!" she said, clapping her hands together. "Mother always called me lazy when I read a book, but I don't care. I dearly love to read."

"As do I," he said with a grin. Taking her hand, he pulled her from the room and went to the end of the hall, opening a door wide. She'd assumed earlier it was an office for him, but no. It was a huge library.

Stepping into the room, he lit a lantern so she could see, even though there was still sunlight streaming into the room. "What do you think?" he asked softly.

"Oh, it's absolutely glorious!" She hurried to the ladder that was on wheels so the highest shelves could be reached. "Now my life is complete, because I have a library with a rolling ladder!"

"It is something to be desired. I'm happy I could fulfill that lifelong dream of yours." He bowed over her hand, kissing it dramatically. "Do you have a favorite book?"

She smiled. "I brought my four favorite books with me. Now I'll have to read all of yours to decide if I like one better than the ones I brought."

"Very good idea." He nodded happily. "Perhaps, though, it would be best if we took our enjoyment of each other up to the bedroom."

She grinned, standing on tiptoe to kiss his cheek. "If you'll give me twenty minutes, I'll be ready for you."

He frowned. "Twenty minutes? That's forever!"

"I believe you'll survive it, if you stand on your rolling ladder, and imagine spinning in it around the room. It will make you happy."

"I suppose it will. Or maybe I'll go steal another piece of cake from the kitchen."

"Is it stealing if it already belongs to you?" she asked, tilting her head to one side curiously.

"It is if I want to pretend to be Robin Hood. I'll steal from the rich, myself, and give to the poor, also myself. I feel poor since you're taking your beautiful presence away from me."

Florence laughed softly. "Twenty minutes."

He nodded. "Twenty minutes."

Hurrying up the stairs, she found the nightclothes she'd put at the top of one of the trunks earlier, and went into the bathroom to ready herself. It was only then she saw how badly her hair had fallen during her nap. Why, her chignon was off to one side, perched precariously above her right ear. She looked a fright, and he'd not only said nothing, but he'd treated her as if she was the most beautiful woman in the world.

He was a good man. There was no other conclusion to make.

She changed into the beautiful garment she'd chosen for her wedding night before taking the pins from her hair to wear it down. She was married to a man who had never seen her hair down, and that was not something that should continue.

As soon as she was finished with her hair, she went back into the bedroom, glad that the two rooms were connected as they were. It made it a great deal easier to move back and forth without venturing into the halls where a servant could possibly see her.

She went to one of her trunks and took out one of the books she'd brought with her, sitting in an armchair, planning to read until Jake joined her.

Of course, she found it almost impossible to focus on the book in front of her—a book of poetry by Elizabeth Barrett Browning. Instead, she thought about what she and Jake would do together, wondering how it would feel.

She imagined her hands on her, and his lips on her flesh, and once again she was aching as she had been after their kisses. What would it feel like when he entered her and began the act that would lead to them having children?

She used the book to fan her face. Her mother would have been so disapproving had she seen her at that moment, but Florence didn't care. She was going to enjoy the marriage bed, no matter how her mother had told her to treat it. "Just spread your legs and let him have his way. Don't move and concentrate on something you enjoy. Perhaps you could recite poetry in your head."

The door opened and the look on Jake's face, told her that her mother's advice would not need to be heeded.

Chapter Four

Jake swallowed hard as he stood staring at the beautiful woman who he had the privilege of calling his wife. He closed the door behind him and leaned against it. He'd courted a few women, but never before had he been in a position of actually making love to one, so he was certain he was as nervous as she must be. But he wasn't about to let that stop him from enjoying his wedding night.

He stopped at the foot of the bed, still watching her. Unbuttoning his suit coat, he took it off and laid it on top of one of her trunks. Then he slowly unbuttoned his shirt, aware that she was watching his every move.

He pulled his shirt off, dropping it on the floor. He'd never had less desire to be neat in his entire life. That left him in just his pants and his under things, but he'd wait to take those off until...well, until he was ready to do so.

Walking to the chair where she sat, holding a book that she obviously wasn't reading, he took the book from her and helped her to her feet. "You are beautiful, Florence."

She smiled nervously, having to remind herself that she was going to be a willing participant of her wedding night and not just lie there with her legs spread as her mother had encouraged.

Reaching out one tentative hand, she felt the muscles of his chest under her fingertips. "What keeps you so fit?" she asked, finding she rather enjoyed touching him. Her body ached where they would soon join, and she found she secretly enjoyed the ache.

He frowned. "I...I do some boxing at a gentleman's club in town."

"I like how you feel," she said softly, surprised that he wasn't touching her as of yet.

"I have a feeling it's going to be mutual," he said, his lips twisting into a smile.

"Feel free," she said, taking another step closer to him and pressing her body against his, with only the thin layer of silk between them. She looked down to see her breasts splayed against his chest, and she smiled. "We look good together."

He groaned, his arms going around her and pulling her up closer against him even as his lips lowered to hers. The kiss was just as passionate as the one they'd shared that afternoon, but with one difference. They didn't have to stop this time.

She felt something hard through the fabric of his slacks, up against her, and she reached down to see what it was. To her surprise he groaned loudly, removing her hand. "Things are going to happen much too quickly if you touch me there."

Looking into his eyes in confusion, she asked, "What am I touching?"

He choked. "You do know how babies are made?" he asked, worried he would have to explain it to her, and he had no desire to stop what they were doing for a conversation.

"I do."

"That's the part of me that will go inside you," he said, thankful the conversation would not be had.

"Oh. It feels bigger than the baby boys I've seen."

He smiled. "It grows as a boy does."

"Oh, I see." She felt stupid for having asked the question, but he seemed to be happy to answer it. She thought once again about what a good man he was.

He pulled her to him and kissed her once more, this time trailing a line of kisses from her mouth, across her cheek, down the side of her neck, and stopping at her cleavage. "I think this needs to come off," he said, pulling at the negligee she wore.

She didn't protest and even stepped back, lifting the offending garment over her head and throwing it on the floor. "Better?" she asked.

"So much better." He stood for a moment just staring at her standing before him in absolutely nothing.

"Well, then it's my turn, isn't it?" Her hands went to the buttons at the front of his trousers, and she carefully liberated each button, watching her fingers as they worked. She couldn't wait to see that part of him that she'd felt against her.

As soon as she pushed his pants down just a little, out sprang something that surprised her more than a little. "Very different than a baby boy's," she said, looking down at it.

He pushed his pants the rest of the way to the floor, making sure to catch his underwear with them. Then he lifted her into his arms, depositing her on the bed. "Maybe we should see how well we fit together," he said, grinning at her.

"Maybe...in a minute."

He sighed. "Why in a minute?"

"I want to feel it first!" She rose to her knees above him and reached out to touch the part of him that had surprised her so. Running her hand over it, she smiled. "It feels like it's stretching to meet me!"

With one motion, he rolled over, pushing her to her back. "Enough of that. I want you to enjoy this just as much as I do," he said. His hand moved between her thighs, and he stroked her there, surprised to find moisture there already. He didn't know if she was ready for him, but he did know he couldn't wait another minute.

He covered her body with his and slowly pressed inside her.

She let out a gasp of pain, and pushed against his shoulder for a moment, but he just kept pushing into her. It was all he could do to hold still as she squirmed under him, but he was able to control himself.

"It shouldn't hurt for long," he said. "And only this once."

The words had him looking into Jake's face, and she could see he was in pain as well. "Are you sure?"

"That's what I've been told. Is it easing now?" he asked, flexing his hips just a little, praying for the self-control to remain still until she was ready for him to move.

She nodded. "I think so."

He moved a hand between them to toy with her, hoping it would make her want more from him.

When she arched up into him, he groaned, knowing his control was spent. He pulled out just a little and sank back inside her.

"That felt good," she said, her voice filled with astonishment.

He pressed his lips to hers once more, as he began the age-old rhythm between men and women. He spent his seed much too quickly, but she didn't seem to mind, curling against him as he rolled to his back.

"That wasn't nearly as bad as I thought it would be," she said softly.

He chuckled. "It'll be better next time."

She sighed contentedly, her head on his chest. "My mother told me to spread my legs and think of something I enjoyed, but all I could think about was how it felt to have you moving inside me. She would be so disappointed in me."

"I'm not," he said softly. "I want you to enjoy what we do together."

"You won't think I'm wanton?" she asked.

"A woman should be wanton when she's in bed with her husband," he said, having no idea if he was telling the truth or not. He only knew what he wanted from his wife.

"So, I don't need to worry about how I act when you're inside me?"

He shook his head. "No, we're just going to enjoy whatever happens, and not worry about what anyone else thinks."

She sighed happily. "I think I'm going to like being married."

He drew her closer and kissed her once more. "Good. Because I'm going to want to do that again. Often."

Giggling, she said, "I don't think I'm going to mind that too much."

He turned down the lamp on his nightstand before closing his eyes. "We should rest so we can do it some more in the morning."

"Sleep sounds wonderful." But there was still that aching between her thighs. She wondered if it would ever go away.

FLORENCE WOKE TO A tickling at her breast. She swatted at it, to hear a laugh, and then looked up, for a moment struggling to remember where she was.

But then it came to her. She was in Cheyenne and the man who was currently touching her was her husband. "Good morning," she said, wondering if he was really wanting to make love again before breakfast.

She soon had her answer to the aching between her thighs. By the time he was finished with her the aching was gone, and she felt as if she was floating on a cloud. Looking over at Jake, she smiled. "I liked it better this morning than last night," she said.

"Good." He was happy he'd finally brought her to fulfillment. Last night when he'd closed his eyes, he'd felt as if he'd done something wrong. Now? He felt like the king of the world.

He laid there holding her for a short while, and then swung his legs out of bed. "I'm hungry!"

"I am too," she sat up in bed, not worried that the sheets were down around her waist and her breasts were visible to him.

He kissed her once more. "I'm going to use the bathroom really quickly, and then you can have it. Take a bath or whatever you feel like doing."

"But I want to eat breakfast with you," she said. "I'll hurry."

While he used the facilities, she found one of the new day dresses from her trousseau, ready to put it on as soon as he was finished. When it was her turn in the bathroom, she washed as quickly and as thoroughly as she could and tugged her clothes on. She was going to love being married to Jake.

She had a feeling Arthur wouldn't have cared if she enjoyed making love, but Jake seemed to be consumed with making her feel good. Oh, what a gloriously wonderful day it was!

When she was dressed, she hurried down the stairs to find him in the parlor. "Are you ready?" she asked.

He nodded. "You look beautiful in that dress," he said.

She laughed. "It's just a simple day dress."

Pursing his lips, he said, "I suppose it is. Oh well. I'll always prefer you without a dress at all."

In the dining room, Mrs. Andrews was just putting breakfast on the table. She'd made eggs, bacon, and toast, and it seemed like a feast to Florence. "Would you like to go for a ride after breakfast?" he asked.

"Shouldn't I start learning my responsibilities today?"

He shook his head. "No, today, you should enjoy being married. Monday is soon enough to learn your responsibilities."

"All right. I do need to have a quick chat with Mrs. Andrews about supper on Tuesday, but I'll be more than happy to just be married for a while."

Breakfast was delicious, and immediately after, Florence ran upstairs to put on her shoes. She was excited to go for a buggy ride with Jake. It would be fun to see the city before she was left to her own devices.

Going outside, she saw Jake speaking with an older man, both of them beside Jake's buggy and horses.

When Florence joined Jake, he said, "This is Mr. Andrews. He's my groundskeeper. Anything Mrs. Andrews doesn't do, Mr. Andrews does."

"It's so nice to meet you, Mr. Andrews," she said.

Mr. Andrews removed his cap and nodded to her. "Mrs. Weatherby. If there's anything I can do for you, let me know."

"I will!" Florence said.

The men finished their conversation and Jake helped Florence into the buggy. "I thought I'd give you a quick tour of the city."

"Oh, I would love that so much!"

He drove them down the main street of the town, showing her the general store, the dressmaker, and the hatmaker. She was fascinated by the town. It was around the same size as Beckham, where she'd come from, but the people dressed so differently. Here, all the men wore cowboy hats, though back home, they'd worn more traditional European hats. And the number of men wearing denim trousers was a shock to her sensibilities.

"I thought we'd try the other restaurant in town for our lunch today," he said. "They have this meal called country-fried steak that I really enjoy and with as much as you liked the hamburger yesterday, I think you'll be happy with a country fried steak as well."

"I'm excited to try it!" She didn't really care what she ate, as long as she was with Jake. It was surprising to her how after just a day in this man's company, her feelings for Arthur had seemed to have completely left her. Jake was a better man by far, and that was very obvious when she compared the two men in her mind.

Pulling up in front of the restaurant, he helped her down from the buggy, and they went into the establishment. This place was even more casual than the first. It appeared if one wanted fine dining in Cheyenne, one must eat at home.

Once they were seated, he gave the waiter their orders, and a full glass of water was placed in front of her. "How soon will it get cold here?" she asked. "It's already going to be September next week." It didn't seem right that school was starting so soon, and it was her first year since she'd finished school.

"Oh, it could snow in September, or it could wait until November. You never know what the weather will do." Jake took a sip of his water, but she'd noticed he hadn't taken his eyes off her since they sat down.

As she looked around the room, she saw plenty of fashionable ladies that were near her age. "Why did you send for a mail-order bride?" she asked. "I would have thought it would be easy for you to find a bride here."

He shrugged. "There are more women out west than women, and I wanted to marry someone with no preconceived notions about me. It seemed like the smartest way to do things."

Some of the ladies were watching them and giggling, which made no sense at all to Florence. Perhaps they knew she was a mail-order bride, and it made them think less of her. She didn't have any urge to meet any of the ladies, which saddened her. She had to find friends here.

When the country fried steak was placed in front of her, she tried it, and smiled. "This is good. I've never had anything like this back east."

"It's a meal invented by the men on cattle drives. They found a way to use the tougher cuts of meat, and they'd still be good."

"Will Mrs. Andrews make this?" she asked, already looking forward to the next time she was able to eat it.

"Yes, she will."

Florence smiled. They'd be able to have it again soon.

Chapter Five

The entire weekend was spent getting to know one another and making love. Florence was thrilled Jake had chosen to take the weekend off, so they could have the time to really feel like they knew one another.

On Tuesday, Florence spent the entire day getting ready for the supper party that evening. She worked with Mr. Andrews to find the best flowers from the garden to garnish the table and the blue parlor, where they would entertain their guests that evening.

She poked her head into Mrs. Andrews's kitchen one time too many, and the woman told her she needed to find something else to do. "I don't know how you expect me to get anything done!"

"Are you sure there isn't something I can do to help?"

"I'm certain. Why don't you go find a book in the library and read for a while?" Mrs. Andrews asked.

"I'll go finish putting my clothing away upstairs," Florence said. "I will need another armoire like the one that's already there."

"There's a furniture maker in town who will be happy to take care of that for you. I'll send Mr. Andrews now."

It was strange to Florence for a woman to call her husband Mr. anything, but she knew her mother had done the same. There was no way she would ever call Jake Mr. Weatherby. No, she felt entirely too close to him to think of him as anything but Jake.

Hurrying to her room to put her belongings away, Florence thought about the wonderful weekend she'd just spent with her new husband. To her, their marriage was absolutely idyllic, and she couldn't imagine feeling any other way than she did at that moment.

Once everything was in its place, she took a long bath before putting on one of her prettiest evening gowns. She wanted to make a good impression on all of the people who would be there that evening.

When Jake came home, he changed into his formal dress while she sat on the edge of the bed talking to him. "I'm nervous," she finally said. "Mrs. Andrews finally kicked me out of the kitchen because I was keeping her from getting anything done."

He chuckled. "There's no reason to be so nervous. You're going to enjoy being around these people," he said.

They were downstairs at five-forty-five, despite his insistence that no one would be early. "Everyone will be here exactly on time," he told her. "I have a feeling they sit in their buggies out front until their watches say six, and then they all come to the door at once."

She grinned. "I like that idea. If only I was a photographer, I'd take a photograph of them just sitting that way."

He chuckled, pulling her to him and kissing her softly. "I'm excited to show you off."

She couldn't stop smiling at him, happy that they were married. She couldn't imagine how any couple could go from the marital bliss she felt with Jake to having a cold marriage like her parents did. No, they would be happy forever. She was convinced of it.

At six, there was a knock on the door, and ten people waiting outside. It was all Florence could do not to laugh. They'd just proved Jake's theory, even though it had sounded a bit demented to her.

As he introduced her to each of the couples, she tried to guess who was whom. She was certain she'd found the railroad man and his wife, and at least one of the ranchers and his wife, but the other three confused her.

The ladies all seemed as if they were looking down their noses at Florence, which surprised her. She would have thought the ladies in town would have wanted to be close to the banker's wife. As little sense as it made to her, she kept her smile firmly planted on her face.

They all went into supper together, and for once, Florence sat at the foot of the table, happy to have a chance to get to know the couple closest to her. "I'm so glad to have the opportunity to get to know all of you," Florence said.

The woman beside her, Mrs. Whitaker, who she'd decided must be the railman's wife, smiled at her in a condescending sort of way. "It's nice to be able to meet the woman who was willing to marry Mr. Weatherby." She shook her head.

"Jake's a wonderful man. Why wouldn't I want to marry him?"

"Oh, you don't know?" Mrs. Whitaker asked. "I was sure someone would have told you by now. Do your servants not gossip like the rest of this town?"

Florence kept her smile in place, but she was furious with this woman. "You are having supper in my husband's home. Do you really think you should be gossiping about him?" She was certain the words would put Mrs. Whitaker in her place.

"Everyone in town knows. It's not gossip any longer."

"Knows what?" Florence asked, ready to kick the woman under the table, but she was certain, Jake would not like it if she did so.

"About his bastard child, of course. The boy and his mother get money from the bank whenever they want it. I saw her in there on Thursday afternoon, getting more money from Mr. Weatherby. I think he gives it to her to keep her quiet, but I don't know why he bothers. Everyone in town knows everything that happened."

Florence smiled sweetly, trying to keep the shock of what she'd just heard off her face. "Don't you think it shows good character to take care of the child and its mother?" She was furious. How dare Jake hide a child and his mother from her? He'd had plenty of time to tell her, and he hadn't. It was like being in the parlor back home with Arthur telling her about his child all over again.

Thankfully, Mrs. Whitaker was shocked by her response and taken aback. "You're not angry?"

"Why would I be angry?" Florence asked. Now she simply had to wait until everyone was gone to kick Jake. And slap his face. And maybe do something else she wasn't able to think of yet. Oh, she could yell at him. That would work. And lock him from their bedroom.

"I...I suppose you don't have to be," Mrs. Whitaker said, though she turned to the woman beside her and began a conversation with her, obviously confused by Florence's reaction to her news.

Florence did everything right for the rest of the evening. She smiled when she was supposed to smile and took Jake's arm as they led the others to the blue parlor. She watched as the men left the room for scotch and cigars, while she was left with the five women, who were all dying to give her more details about her husband's illegitimate child.

He could have warned her. Then she wouldn't be quite so angry. She also would never have trusted him for slept with him.

"Pamela told you about your husband's bastard at supper, I guess," Mrs. Smith said. Florence had pegged her as one of the rancher's wives.

"Yes, she did. What glorious news. A child to love."

The other women seemed confused, and they spoke about other things for the rest of the evening, while Florence thought about the ways she was going to hurt Jake. How dare he!

Jake and Florence said a polite goodnight to their guests at the door that evening, and she turned to go upstairs. As she was climbing, he said, "I'll be up in five minutes."

"Not in my bed, you won't!" Florence continued climbing, having no desire to even look at the man. She had never been this angry in her life, and she wasn't about to talk to him and say things she probably wouldn't regret later.

He was asking her what was wrong as she opened the door to the bedroom and locked it behind her. Then she went into the bathroom and locked that door as well. There was no way he could get in.

She changed into a nightgown that covered her from her neck to her ankles, the kind she'd worn her entire life before marrying and climbed into bed. She was reading one of the history books she'd found in his library when she heard a key in the door, and it opened.

Instead of looking at him, she continued reading her book. When he undressed and got into bed beside her, she took her book and walked across the hall to one of the guest bedrooms. He didn't deserve to have her in the same bed with him.

Jake followed her into the other bedroom. "What is wrong with you?" he asked. He was getting annoyed with the way she wouldn't look at him or talk to him.

"Mrs. Whitaker told me about your son tonight and that you pay his mother to keep quiet, though everyone knows the truth. I left Beckham to not be embroiled in a scandal with my philandering fiancé and his whore. I will not be part of a scandal with your whore here." She never looked at him, and her words sounded much calmer than she felt inside.

He stood staring at her for a minute before nodding once and shutting the door to her room and going back to his own. She didn't deserve to hear the truth.

As soon as he was gone, Florence gave up all pretenses of reading and closed her eyes and sobbed. It was bad enough when it had happened with Arthur, but she hadn't had the same feelings for Arthur she had for Jake.

In less than a week, she'd fallen in love with him, and now she would spend the rest of her life being a laughingstock. Jake was worse than Arthur, because at least Arthur had the courage to tell her about his whore himself. Jake hadn't bothered.

Florence slept late the following day, waking up to red-rimmed eyes. When she went downstairs for breakfast, Mrs. Andrews eyed her curiously. "Did something bad happen at the party last night?" she finally asked.

"Not in the way you're thinking," Florence said. "Mrs. Whitaker told me about Jake's bastard."

Mrs. Andrews's eyes widened. "Did you tell Jake why you're so upset?"

Florence nodded. "He should have told me about his bastard and the boy's whore mother himself."

Mrs. Andrews gave Florence a furious look. "I do hope he'll find some way to forgive you, but I'm not certain it will happen. I liked you before this morning." With that, Mrs. Andrews left the room, and Florence wondered how Mrs. Andrews could possibly take Jake's side in the matter. There was right and there was wrong, and Jake was very obviously on the side of wrong.

Florence spent the day in her room, reading. She had no desire to be seen in public. Now she understood the laughter at the restaurant on Friday. He could have at least told her she would be laughed at wherever she went.

The more she thought about it, the more angry she became. She had been treated like garbage, and she had no desire to even look at her husband again.

Jake didn't come home for supper that night, and she didn't see him again until the following morning. There was no doubt in her mind he'd been with his whore, while she was at home, waiting for him. The man, who had seemed like the perfect man for her, had turned out to be the kind of man she had tried to escape by marrying him. There was irony there that she didn't care to contemplate.

At breakfast, neither looked at the other. He was angry with her just as she was with him. It made no sense to her that she would be the object of his anger. He read his newspaper while they ate, but before he left, he said, "We're going to the home of one of my associates for supper on Friday. Dress accordingly."

Those were the only words either of them spoke over breakfast, and she wanted to throw her eggs at him, but he had the newspaper in front of him. What was the point when her aim would miss its target, even though it would be true?

Florence decided to venture out that afternoon. She wanted to take a gift to supper at his associates house to thank them for the meal, even though no one had done that for them. She knew what was correct and mannerly.

At the store, she saw a young woman with a boy of about three. The boy asked for candy, but his mother told him she didn't have the money to waste. Florence purchased several pieces of the penny candy and had them put into a bag, which she offered to his mother. "Then you won't have to deny him the next time he asks," Florence said sweetly, hoping to make a friend of the young woman.

"Thank you, Miss..."

"Mrs. Weatherby," Florence said, wishing she could let the store swallow her up rather than admit she'd married Jake.

"You must be Jake's wife," the girl said.

Florence nodded, waiting to hear even more gossip about her husband.

Instead, the girl glared at her, throwing the bag of candy back in her face. "Jake is a good man, and you've treated him like he's nothing. I hope you eat all that candy and it rots your teeth!" She took the boy's hand and pulled him out of the store crying, wondering what was wrong with the girl.

Another lady, old enough to be Florence's mother was watching. "You just made enemies of the mother of your husband's child," the woman said. "I'd be more careful in future if I were you."

Florence closed her eyes. How could the girl say Jake was a good man when he'd refused to marry her when she was expecting his child? It made no sense at all.

Instead of purchasing something, Florence hurried out onto the sidewalk to see if she could spot the woman. When she did, she began following her. There was a truth that she wasn't completely understanding, and she needed to know what it was.

Finally the woman and her son walked into an old, dilapidated house. Florence went to the door and knocked loudly.

When the other woman answered the door, Florence said, "There's more to the story than I know, apparently. Would you tell me?"

The girl stood glaring at her for a moment, and then she nodded, opening the door wider. "Let me just put Jesse down for his nap."

Florence stood for a moment, thinking. Wasn't Jesse Jake's brother's name?

"I'm Kate by the way," the woman said as she took a seat in a chair, not inviting Florence to do the same.

"It's nice to meet you, Kate," Florence said, her manners automatically kicking in.

"I was engaged to Jesse, Jake's brother. Well, first Jake and I courted, but I realized pretty quickly that it was his brother I had feelings for. Jesse and I anticipated our vows by a week, thinking it wouldn't matter if we had a child who was only an eight-and-a-half-month baby." She shook her head.

"Oh!" Florence began to understand, and realized she owed her husband a huge apology.

Kate nodded. "I see you're following my meaning. Jesse died the day before we were to be married. When I found out a short while later that I was expecting, Jake offered to marry me. When I told him no, he insisted on setting up a fund to help the baby and me."

"I was told the money was to keep you quiet."

"No, the money was to help me raise his nephew, and he's helped me in every way he can. I was keeping all the money in an account for Jesse when he gets older, but my roof caved in, and I needed a little, which is why I met with Jake on Thursday."

"I see," Florence said softly.

"Now, please leave my house, and never again use me as a reason to be cruel to Jake."

Florence nodded, feeling like a heel. She left the house and hurried home. She had some serious apologizing to do.

Chapter Six

Florence waited in the parlor for Jake to come home, intending to apologize to him immediately and praying he would find it in his heart to forgive her for her treatment of him, even though she knew she didn't deserve to be forgiven. She'd taken out her anger at Arthur on him, and she'd never even had proof.

Sitting in the parlor with a book on her lap, she listened for the door, planning to tell him right away how sorry she was and how much she cared for him and didn't want their marriage to fail.

As soon as she heard the door, she jumped to her feet and rushed into the hallway. "Can we talk?" she asked.

He raised an eyebrow. "I thought you already had me figured out. Why would you want to talk? I don't think there's anything left to say, is there?"

"I'm sorry," she said. "If you'll come into the parlor with me, I'll give you a proper apology, on my knees if necessary."

"Or I can buy you a train ticket back to Massachusetts. That would work as well, don't you think?"

"No, I don't. I won't go back there."

"Because you'll be laughed at? Poor Florence. So mistreated by the men in her life."

Florence shook her head. "One man mistreated me, but never you. You gave me nothing but affection, and in turn, I was terrible to you."

"Yes, you were. I'm sorry, but an apology isn't enough right now. I treated you like a queen."

"You did. And I threw it back into your face like some sort of shrew. I'll do whatever it takes to get you to forgive me."

"Good luck with that." Jake knew he was being awful, but he felt that she deserved it. Never had he done a single thing to make her think he was less than trustworthy, and he would have told her the full truth if she'd only asked. But she'd drawn her own conclusions—the same conclusions everyone else in town had drawn. He'd been certain by bringing in a lady from the east to marry, there would be no more talk of his infidelities, and even if there was, he'd have a wife to side with him.

He went up the stairs to change for supper, not bothering to worry about how she was feeling. He'd spent altogether too much time being the perfect husband. Now he could be the scorned husband.

At supper, she sat at the foot of the table, where she'd only sat one night before, and she toyed with her food, eating very little. He noticed, but he said nothing. She needed to learn a lesson. And he was going to have to be her teacher whether he liked it or not.

Florence stared down at her food, wondering what she could do to convince him that she was truly contrite, and she would never believe anything negative about him again. She'd definitely learned her lesson.

When she'd finished pushing the food around on her plate, she asked, "May I move back into our bedroom?"

He shrugged. "I don't care where you sleep."

She took the verbal jab right to the jaw, but she nodded. "I'll move my things back after supper then."

Mrs. Andrews came into the room, obviously unhappy with Florence. "I made your favorite dessert," she said softly to Jake.

He smiled. "I'd like a big slice of caramel apple pie."

Mrs. Andrews gazed at Florence, her voice stiff. "And you, Mrs. Weatherby?"

Florence shook her head. "I believe I'll skip dessert tonight." As soon as Mrs. Andrews had gone back to the kitchen, Florence went upstairs to start the process of moving back to his bedroom.

She knew she didn't deserve the pleasure of sleeping with him, but perhaps she could get him to soften toward her just a little.

She was certain she should feel guilty for moving back to his bed to try and get him to forgive her, but she didn't know what else to do. She knew she'd made a true mess of her marriage after only a week, but she prayed something could be done to make things better.

She spent the evening moving things back into his bedroom and working on getting the last of her clothes put away. Jake had promised he'd get her another armoire, but she had no idea when he'd actually do it, and she couldn't hang everything until she had it.

She put on a pretty negligee when it was close to bedtime, and slid into bed, reading one of the history books she'd found in his library. Their library. She was convinced their marriage would last, and that meant she had to stop thinking of everything as his and not theirs.

When he joined her a long while later, he glanced in her direction, and his eyes narrowed. "What are you doing?" he asked, noting all the skin that was exposed by her choice of nightwear.

Knowing exactly what he meant, but choosing to ignore it, she said, "Reading one of the history books from your library. I don't usually enjoy nonfiction, but I love to read history books for whatever reason. This one is on the French Revolution."

"I'm familiar with the book." He stared at her for a moment, wondering if she could truly be as dense as she was acting, but he knew better. They'd had conversations about such a variety of topics, he knew she was intelligent.

Finally, he decided to take what was being offered. Even though he was annoyed with her, they were married and he had marital rights. Not that he'd ever take them without her approval. He didn't think like men of the past did. He'd thought their marriage was perfect just days before.

He quickly stripped down to his altogether and slipped into the bed with her. Removing the book from her hands, he placed it on the table on his side of the bed. Then he turned to her, pulling her against him. "This doesn't mean I forgive you," he said softly, needing to make it clear to her this didn't fix the problems in their marriage.

"I know." She'd hoped it could help to fix things, though. Being touched by him would certainly make her feel closer to him, and that's all she was looking for at the moment.

Their lovemaking that night wasn't as tender as it had been, but he wasn't rough with her either. He treated her the way he'd planned to treat whoever stepped off the train to be his wife. Never had he imagined she would be someone he could actually care about.

They fell asleep entwined in each other's arms, with her hoping things were better, and him wondering if he'd just made a huge mistake.

The following evening was supper at Jake's business associate's house. Florence dressed carefully, trying to look her absolute best for the evening. She'd hated when her mother had made her dress with appearance in mind, and now she found herself doing it to please Jake. At that moment, she would do anything to please Jake.

She wore a beautiful gown of sky blue that matched her eyes perfectly. It was the only item she'd allowed her mother to choose for her, and she knew she looked better in it than in any of the dresses she'd chosen. Her mother had exquisite taste, and she wished she'd allowed her to choose more for her. Of course, it was easy to know what to do in hindsight.

When Florence descended the stairs to find Jake at the bottom of them, she smiled as sweetly as she knew how. It was hard knowing they were at odds with one another.

"You look beautiful," he said softly when she reached the entryway where he waited for her.

"Thank you." She vowed to write her mother the next day and ask her to choose more evening gowns. The dressmaker in Beckham still had her measurements.

His buggy was waiting out front, and he handed her up and made certain she was comfortable. "I don't want anyone in town to know there's a problem between us," he said, staring straight ahead. "I would appreciate it if you made it appear as if you were madly in love with me."

"I guess I'll just be myself then."

He refused to react to her statement, though it made him feel good. He couldn't let her know the power she had over him after the way she'd treated him. She couldn't truly be trusted.

When they reached the house of his associate, it was a large house, though not as large as Jake's. He helped her down and they walked to the door. "Is it exactly time to knock?" she whispered.

His mouth tilted as he remembered what he'd told her the other night. He wanted to banter with her and enjoy it, but he wasn't certain it was the right thing to do. He couldn't risk completely losing his heart to her, though he was afraid the battle was mostly over, and she'd emerged triumphant.

He knocked loudly, unable to resist pulling out his pocket watch, and showing her, it was five minutes til time to knock. "Are we being rebels then?"

He bit back his laughter, not wanting her to know how much her presence and easy banter pleased him.

The lady of the house answered the door, and she warmly welcomed both of them. Jake introduced her. "Mrs. Brooks, this is my wife, Florence. Florence, this is Mrs. Brooks." Jake was aware that Mrs. Brooks was one of the women who gossiped about him, but he'd risen above it for three years. He was certain Florence could follow his lead and do the same.

"Come into the parlor," Mrs. Brooks said. "You're a little early, but I'm sure the others will be here momentarily."

She led them to an immaculate parlor, and then left when there was another knock on the door. "She said we were early. She noticed. Do you think she was holding up a pocket watch and waiting for the first people to knock? Oh, she must think us absolute cads for arriving early!" Florence rested the back of her wrist against her forehead.

He couldn't help but laugh. "Shhh."

They were joined by five other couples before they were led into supper. She was seated between two women she'd barely met and readied herself for another supper. At least she was used to moving in the type of circles she was finding herself in.

The woman to her right dropped her voice. "How does it feel to know your husband has a bastard?" she asked.

Florence wasn't certain why the women of this town were so ready to attack her, but she smiled. "Oh, it feels good. The little boy is just adorable, and his mother very sweet. I'm pleased to know them."

"I..." Mrs. White stared at her in shock. "It doesn't bother you?"

Florence lifted one shoulder in a shrug. "I don't know why it would. He didn't meet me until last week. Why should I be bothered by what happened before we were married?"

Jake was busy having his own conversations, and the women all seemed to talk amongst themselves, but Florence wasn't included again. Surely the women of this town had more to talk about than Jake.

"This town is quite rugged, don't you think?" Florence asked the table in general. "Are there any parks where I may go to walk in the afternoons?"

The other women all remained silent, but Mr. White smiled at her. "There is a lovely park just at the end of your street. If you go out your front door, take a right, and walk for a few minutes. You'll find it there. Many young mothers take their children there to get some fresh air."

"Oh, I'll have to walk there on Monday. Well, if I can't convince Jake we need to go tomorrow, of course. I do prefer not to leave the house without him at my side."

"And I would rather walk with you, my dear. We'll have to go tomorrow. I'd say Sunday, but we were naughty and skipped church last week, so we must go there to worship on Sunday."

"That sounds just wonderful. I'll have Mrs. Andrews pack us a picnic lunch."

Mrs. White looked at Florence. "A walk in the park is something we did often years ago. When Mr. White was courting me of course. Since we've married there have been few romantic gestures."

"Oh, how sad. Jake and I really enjoy being together, and he's ever so romantic. My heart leaps with joy every time he smiles at me. I do hope our honeymoon is never over."

Jake couldn't help but smile at Florence's words. She was doing just as he'd asked and acting as if everything was perfect between them. And for a moment, it was as if their fight earlier in the week had never happened.

Unfortunately, the feeling left quickly. He'd married a wife who could act perfect in public, and that's what he'd requested. Though she was perfect in other ways as well...

Chapter Seven

On the way home that evening, Jake grinned at Florence, making her feel as if she'd just climbed the tallest mountain in the world. "I heard how you responded when Mrs. White asked how you felt about Jesse, and that was absolutely perfect. Thank you."

"Of course. I shouldn't have ever reacted any differently."

"And I appreciate that you made me sound like the most romantic husband in the world, even though I know I'm not."

Florence sighed. "You were the most romantic husband in the world until I messed everything up between us. I wish I could say the right thing to make you forgive me."

"It's not a matter of forgiveness," he said. "It's a matter of trust. I don't feel like I can trust you anymore."

"I'll do everything I can to make you trust me again. I really am sorry I blew it. I just...well, there's no excuse for the way I acted."

"What were you going to say?" he asked.

"Well, I ended up out here because the man I was supposed to marry got someone else pregnant while we were engaged. I'd known him for years and trusted him implicitly. Then I found out I was all wrong for doing so. I'd known you for five days, and I didn't have a hard time believing it." She shook her head. "I was wrong, and I hope that someday, I can make it up to you."

"I think I can understand how you made the leap, but the next time someone comes to you and says I did something wrong, will you believe that as well?"

"I feel pretty confident in you now. But I can't promise I won't believe something. I can only promise I'll ask you about it and not act like a child because someone dared to say something bad about you." Florence sighed.

"Well, we'll have to see what happens then, won't we?" He felt good about the fact that she hadn't claimed she'd always believe him. At least she was being as truthful as she could be.

Early the following morning, Florence went to talk to Mrs. Andrews. "I know you don't think much of me now, but I do love Jake, and I'll convince you both...eventually. In the meantime, would you make us a picnic lunch to have at the park today?"

Mrs. Andrews studied her for a moment. "I'm glad you're making an effort. I've never seen him as happy as he was the first few days you were married."

"Thank you for saying that. I feel as though I've ruined my marriage only five days into it."

"He's a good man. He'll learn to trust you again." Mrs. Andrews pursed her lips. "I'll get a picnic lunch ready. Would noon be acceptable?"

"Oh, yes. Thank you!" Florence hurried back up the stairs, hoping she'd seen Jake before he'd dressed so she could let him know the picnic was being prepared.

When she entered their room, he was still sleeping, and he looked so...well, perfect was the only word that came to mind. He looked perfect to her. She took the book from his nightstand and sat down in the armchair to read it, without lighting any lamps. The sun streaming into the room was enough to see by.

As she read, she was very aware of him sleeping a short distance from her, and she hoped he would be awake in time for their picnic. What if he'd just agreed to it because people had been listening? Either way, she'd do all she could to talk him into it.

When he finally woke, it was already after ten. "Are you feeling all right?" she asked.

He looked at her for a moment, surprised to see her in the room with him. "I tend to sleep in on Saturdays," he said. "We had some late nights this week, and it helps me catch up. There's a musical showing in town tonight I want to take you to. All of the upper class will be there, and the more I appear with you, the better it will be. You're helping my reputation a great deal."

"Why don't you just tell everyone the child isn't yours?"

He shrugged. "Because he's my nephew, and he looks like me. I'll do anything I can to make life more comfortable for him and Kate. Kate loved Jesse with everything inside her, as I did. I feel I should keep her close."

"I can understand that. I had Mrs. Andrews ready a picnic for us. Are you still willing to go to the park?"

He nodded. "Everything we do together publicly is good for my reputation. And good for us," he added softly.

She moved to him and sat beside him on the bed. "I'm glad you're not sending me back to Massachusetts. I know I don't deserve to stay, but I'm thankful you're letting me."

He put an arm around her and pulled her close. "I'm thankful you're willing to face people who say terrible things about me without telling them the truth. This town has not been kind to me since my brother died, and I feel as if I finally have someone in my corner." He kissed her softly. "Now, let me get ready for that picnic. Do you mind if I wear jeans?"

She grinned. "I'd like that." She'd noticed jeans seemed to fit tighter than other trousers, and she liked the idea of how he'd look in them.

She put on one of her day dresses that was perfect for sitting on the ground and hurried down to see if Mrs. Andrews would include a blanket for them to sit on.

To her surprise, she found a formal picnic basket on the counter, with a blanket in one spot and plates and cutlery included. This would be a very nice picnic.

Florence thought for a moment about inviting Kate and Jesse, but then decided she would do that during the week. It would be nice to get to know the other woman and her child. They were Jake's family after all.

"Thank you for including a picnic," Florence said, moving to kiss Mrs. Andrews on the cheek. "And thank you for giving me another chance."

Mrs. Andrews smiled. "Jake said he was taking you to the theater for a musical this evening. Do you know if it's dinner theater or if you'll be eating out beforehand?"

"I don't. Let me run and ask him for you. That way you won't spend your day cooking when you could be spending it with Mr. Andrews."

"Thank you," Mrs. Andrews said, looking surprised.

Florence hurried back up the stairs to ask Jake about supper. "Mrs. Andrews wants to know if we're attending a dinner theater, eating out before the performance, or eating at home this evening?"

Jake was standing in his jeans, pulling on a casual button-down shirt. "It's dinner theater."

"I'll run and tell her."

Jake shook his head, laughing at his wife running up and down the stairs to make it easier on his housekeeper. She may have said some things she shouldn't have, but she was certainly endearing herself to him.

She was back with him a short while later. "She's going to leave after she finishes our lunch and cleans up then," Florence said.

"I think she should. I wish I had extra tickets for the theater tonight for her and Mr. Andrews."

"Oh, we should do something like that for them for Christmas."

"I'd like that a lot. I think a lot of them, and I never can pick out the right gift."

"I'll help," Florence offered. "It's actually something I do quite well."

"See? You're going to be useful after all."

She resisted the urge to stick her tongue out at him. He was simply being difficult. But as she wasn't sticking her tongue out at him, she realized that they were bantering as they had at first. He'd forgiven her. She knew he didn't trust her yet, but she felt they could work through that.

Soon, she was holding onto his arm, as he carried the picnic basket toward the park. As they walked, she felt safe and secure, knowing he would take care of her. He was a good man, which was evidenced by how he took care of Kate and Jesse. She couldn't believe she'd ever thought he was a bad man because of Jesse.

As they walked, she asked, "What musical are we going to see tonight?"

"It's a musical comedy called *Shop Girl*. It's all the rage in New York and London. I think we'll both enjoy it."

"Have you seen it?" she asked.

"No, tonight is opening night. I was dearly hoping you would love the theater as much as I do."

"I've seen a couple of shows on Broadway with my parents, but that's the only experience I have of the theater. My mother didn't consider the small theater in Beckham worth going to."

He shook his head. "I'll try any theater three times. If the first two plays are bad, I'll give it one more shot. If all three are bad, then I'm finished."

"I like that plan. Have you been to this theater before?" she asked.

"Every time there's a new play, I try to make it on opening night. I used to go with my family, and then I went with my brother. The past few years, I've been going alone. I do love theater after all."

"Is it a good theater?" she asked.

"It's all right. I've been to several plays on Broadway, and they were much better, but this is what I can watch here in town. If I want a good theater, I'll take a week off and take the train to Seattle. They have a wonderful opera house there with fabulous acoustics."

"Oh! That sounds like fun!"

He smiled. "Maybe we can plan a trip then."

"I'd like that."

When they reached the park, there were ladies with baby carriages, and a few young couples picnicking in the grass. Florence was excited to be able to join them and told herself she would come often as long as the weather held.

She spread the blanket, and he put the basket down on top of it. Then she dug through the basket and served them each a plate and smiled when she saw a jar of lemonade had been included, pouring them each a glass.

As they ate, she asked, "Would you mind if I invited Kate and Jesse over for lunch one day? I think it would go far to show how innocent you are if I spent time with them when you were working."

He frowned for a moment. "Would you be doing it to prove to the world I was innocent for your reputation? Or to make things easier for me in town?" he asked. He hated being skeptical, but they didn't have good history in this regard.

"To make things easier for you. Now that I know it's not true, I truly don't care what people say to or about me."

"Then invite them. Jesse is a sweet boy, and I asked them to move in with me when he was first born, but Kate wouldn't ruin my reputation that way. Of course, it was ruined anyway."

Florence thought about it for a moment. "With me there, people may think it's strange if they live with us, but it wouldn't be as damaging to you or her reputation. I could invite them."

He stared at her for a moment, smiling a little. "You'd do that?"

"I would."

"I don't like the idea because I don't think we'd have the privacy newlyweds need. And you'd have to learn to be much quieter..."

Florence blushed. "All right. How does Kate support them?"

"Well, I'm sure you know I help when needed, but mainly she sews shirts for me. Women won't use her as a seamstress because she's undesirable, but men don't seem to care."

"I see. I was thinking of having my mother order a few more dresses for me because she's much better at knowing what will look best on me, but if Kate could help, I'd happily commission her to sew a few dresses."

He raised an eyebrow but then nodded. "That would help her, I would think."

"I'll go see her then. And I'll wear the dresses and if I'm asked where they came from, I'll shout it from the rooftops. What is Kate's last name?" she asked.

"Perry. Thank you for wanting to help them."

"Of course I do. I don't think anticipating your vows by a few days warrants being shunned for the rest of your life."

"Would you have anticipated your vows?" he asked.

She thought about it for a moment but eventually shook her head. "I don't think so. My mother convinced me I would go straight to hell if I did something like that. Like, I would have immediately ceased to draw breath. Besides, I'm glad it was special for us the way it was."

He studied her. "You confuse me at times, Florence. You were so angry with me, and now you're acting like all is good, and you want to be Kate's friend."

Florence smiled. "I understand why Kate is where she is. I would never have reacted the way I did if Arthur hadn't cheated on me. It was still too fresh in my mind. Of course, he's fading away into distant memories as I can only think of you."

"You don't still love him?"

She shrugged. "I don't think I ever did. He was familiar. He courted me all through my last year of school, and my parents approved of him. But he didn't make me feel what I feel when you kiss me."

"Is that so?" he asked, his eyes twinkling a little.

She nodded emphatically. "Oh yes. I feel like you've turned me into a different person altogether. When you're gone during the day, I think about how I feel when you touch me." Florence knew she shouldn't be so forthright with her thoughts and feelings, but she didn't care. She enjoyed his touch, and if he hadn't figured that out yet, then there was something wrong with his powers of observation.

He reached for her hand and brought it to his lips, brushing a soft kiss on it. "I want to go home."

"Why?" she asked, fearing she'd angered him somehow.

"Because I want to remember what it feels like to have you writhing in my arms. I want to make love with you in the middle of the day and not care if someone finds out."

She smiled. "I'd like that too, but I'd rather people didn't know when we made love."

He stood and started to repack the picnic on his own, and she smiled. "I thought your bottom would look nice in your jeans."

He shook his head. "Help me pack this thing. And stop looking at my bottom. I wish we'd driven so we could get home faster."

She giggled. "I think we can make it back quickly. Want to race?"

"You are going to be the death of me, Florence Weatherby."

"We'll both die happy."

Chapter Eight

The theater was crowded, and Florence felt a little lost in it. Thankfully, Jake led her to a private box at the top, making her feel a little safer. Their meal was brought to them just before the play started, and Florence smiled, thanking the server.

"I've noticed you do that. Do you always thank people who are paid to serve you?" he asked.

She nodded. "I think I developed the habit because my mother told me to stop." She shrugged. "Sometimes I did anything I could to make her crazy."

He chuckled. "And why did you do that?"

"She was very controlling. I wasn't allowed to have friends she didn't first approve. I had to go to balls every time there was one in Beckham, and often she took me into Boston for them. I wanted to wait until I was a little older to marry, but when Arthur asked my father for my hand, my mother made it clear that I would say yes, whether I liked it or not. My dresses had to be white for all dances because I was available and unmarried. Many of the things she did made no sense to me at all, but I still did as I was told. Except for thanking servants. That was something she couldn't stop me from doing."

He shook his head. "I may need to watch for little things you do to make me crazy."

"It's not the same," she said, smiling. "Mother controlled me because she felt like everything else in her life was out of her control. You don't try to control me, and I thank you for that."

"I have never felt the need to control anyone," he said softly.

"I'm glad," she responded. "The way my mother was with me, even drove my father out of his mind. I heard them yelling at night a few times."

He didn't respond because the curtain came up and the musical started.

She was on the edge of her seat watching everything that happened on the stage. She almost forgot she was supposed to be eating, but she forced herself to finish her meal so she wouldn't have to find something for herself later. She was not a cook by any stretch of the imagination.

At the intermission, she stood. "I need to find the ladies' room."

He pointed toward the way they'd come in. "Just go down those stairs and take a right."

She hurried from the box, not wanting to miss a single word of the second half. It had been far too long since her mother had allowed her to attend a theater. She was happy Jake was a theater lover though because it meant she could go often.

In the ladies' room, there was a group of women who were obviously wealthy. They wore silk gowns and stood together, looking down their noses at others. She said nothing, but got into line behind them.

"And who are you?" one of the women asked, sizing her up with a look.

"I'm Florence Weatherby. And you are?"

"Janice Wilson. Wife of George Wilson."

"It's nice to meet you. I haven't heard of George yet, but I've only been in town a little over a week."

"And you married Jake Weatherby?" the woman asked.

Florence nodded, waiting to hear all the reasons she shouldn't have married Jake. It was amazing how many of the women in town seemed to think they should be the ones who controlled his life. "Yes, I married Jake last Thursday."

"He's a wonderful man, isn't he?" Mrs. Wilson asked. "My George was about to lose his ranch last year, and Jake did everything he could to help him. I was afraid we'd have to move into a hovel, but Jake saved the day. I don't care what anyone says about him."

Florence smiled. "He is a wonderful man. All I hear is gossip about him, but I know who he is, and I'm proud to be his wife."

"As you should be," Mrs. Wilson said.

The women she'd been talking with had all gotten quiet, but Florence was thrilled to have found just one ally in town. "Your husband is a rancher then?" Florence asked.

"He is. Last year was a bad year, but he's still the most successful rancher in this part of Wyoming."

"I hope we'll see more of each other."

"I do too, dear."

When Mrs. Wilson disappeared into the ladies' room, one of her companions gave Florence a look that told her the other woman didn't hold the same opinions as Mrs. Wilson. Florence didn't care though. It was nice to see someone in town understood what a wonderful person her husband was.

When she returned to the box, Mr. And Mrs. Wilson were there, talking to Jake. As soon as Florence was there, Jake introduced her to Mr. Wilson. "I understand you met Mrs. Wilson already," he said.

"Yes, I did. We should have them over to supper," Florence said.

Jake smiled. "I'd like that. Maybe Wednesday evening?"

Mr. Wilson shook his head. "No, let us host you. I have to be up before five every morning, and tomorrow's going to be difficult enough. Can't do that twice in one week." He clapped Jake on the back. "We can't all keep banker's hours."

"Wednesday night at your house then," Jake agreed.

"Can we bring anything?" Florence asked Mrs. Wilson. "Since you're hosting us without planning to?"

Mrs. Wilson shook her head. "I'll take care of everything."

"I look forward to seeing you then," Florence said, happy to have found a like-minded woman in town.

As the other couple left their box, Florence said, "I like her!"

Jake chuckled. "You sound shocked you like someone in this town."

"Before today, I'd only met women who wanted to gossip about you. Mrs. Wilson told me she didn't care what anyone said about you and that you're a good man."

"Well, then I'll like her too." He was surprised Florence felt defensive toward him. He'd dealt with the rumors for so long, he didn't care anymore, but she obviously did. It was odd, but he knew she was a good person, despite how she'd treated him.

After the musical, they drove home in the brisk night air. Florence wanted to spin in a circle, dancing, while singing some of the songs that had been part of the musical.

Of course, she couldn't carry a tune in a bucket, and she knew better than singing in front of her husband. No, he didn't need to hear her caterwauling.

Once they reached the house, she hurried inside, wanting to dress for bed. There was something magical that happened when Jake touched her, and she was going to enjoy every second with him.

She hurried into the kitchen and found some of the cookies that had been baked for the picnic, put them on a plate, and carried them upstairs. Who was to say they couldn't have a picnic on their bed consisting of just cookies? There was no one to stop them, and to Florence, they would be the perfect ending to a wonderful day.

When he got upstairs, he saw her with the cookies, and laughed. "Are we having a party of some sort?"

She grinned. "I've had the most wonderful day. My husband took me for a picnic, and then dinner while watching a musical. I'm practically walking on air. I thought it would be good if we ended the day the same way we've lived it."

"I cannot complain about that at all," he said.

She was already ready for bed, and he quickly stripped down to just his drawers. He didn't feel right eating completely naked, and he wasn't sure why. He'd have to think about that later.

"What did you think of the musical?" she asked.

"Oh, I thought it was wonderful. I take it you enjoyed it."

"So much! I'm so glad we have that interest in common. And I love the idea of spending some time in Seattle seeing musicals there as well."

"You're pretty special. I hope you know that."

"Not really," she said. "I wish I was a better person."

"Don't we all? I look in a mirror, and I see only my faults. You look in a mirror and see your own faults. But I look at you, and I see someone who truly makes me happy."

She smiled, lifting a cookie to his lips. "You make me happy as well, Jake. I hope you can see that."

SUNDAY MORNING, THEY went to church. The service wasn't until ten, and it felt like they were lazy as they didn't wake until after eight. Florence dressed in one of her church dresses, while Jake put on one of his business suits. She'd only seen him wear something else one time, which was odd to her. But she supposed her father had been the same.

When they entered the church, she was excited to meet more people, feeling good about what Mrs. Wilson had said the night before.

As she looked around the church, most of the women turned away from her as if she was a pariah. She didn't know why they were treating her badly, but she decided she wouldn't give them the time of day.

After a moment, she spotted Kate off in a back corner of the building with little Jesse. She made a beeline toward them, keeping her voice loud as she spoke to her. "It's so good to see you again, Kate. I was hoping I could have you make a few dresses for me."

Kate's eyes widened, but she nodded. "Yes, of course."

"I'll need your help picking a pattern and fabric that would look good on me," Florence said. "My mother always picked the right clothes for me, but I don't have her eye."

"I'd be happy to help!" Kate said.

"Why don't you and Jesse come for lunch on Monday, and we can talk about what I'd like after?"

Kate bit her lip, obviously wanting the business. "Jesse naps right after lunch..."

"He can nap there. I'm certain I'll keep you busy for his entire nap. I want several new evening gowns."

"That would be wonderful then. I look forward to seeing you around noon."

"Would you mind if we sat with you?" Florence asked. If she was going to dispel rumors, she couldn't think of a better way of doing it.

Kate scooted over, making room for Florence and Jake. "Jake usually sits in his family pew in the front..."

"Then you should join us there," Florence said. "I don't really care where we sit."

"I'm more comfortable back here," Kate said quietly.

"Then this is where we'll sit," Florence said, sitting next to the older woman. She looked past her and smiled at Jesse. "Good morning, Jesse."

Jesse popped his thumb from his mouth and smiled. "Hello."

That day's sermon was on forgiveness, and Florence felt that Kate had forgiven her. She was thrilled to have her and Mrs. Wilson she felt like she could talk to. And Mrs. Andrews, of course. She'd been lonesome for home and her best friend there, but now, building friendships here felt good.

After the sermon, Mrs. Whitaker pulled her aside. "It's not a good idea for you to spend time with her. We all know she's a fallen woman."

Florence smiled at the other woman. "She's my friend. I don't care if she's fallen, risen, or sideways."

"You'll share in her reputation if you continue this nonsense."

Florence shrugged. "I'd rather spend time with someone who made a mistake than the person who is eternally looking down on her for it." She looked over her shoulder to see Kate stand and pick up Jesse, who had been complaining he was hungry for a while. "If you'll excuse me, I'd rather talk to my friend."

"Can I help in any way?" Florence asked.

"No, I'll carry him home. He's just hungry."

"Why don't you come and have lunch with us? Both of you, of course." Florence couldn't help but wonder where Kate's family was. They should be with her as she faced the people who had been so cruel to her.

Kate smiled. "I don't think Jesse is up for company. Church is hard for us."

"I understand that. I'll see you tomorrow then?"

"I'll be there, and I'll bring my book of styles."

Florence was surprised the woman had a book of styles, since she mostly sewed men's shirts. She couldn't wait to see it though.

She left the church on Jake's arm, and he shook his head at her. "I can't believe you did that."

"Why not? She's the mother of your nephew, so she'll be my friend. It's as simple as that."

"Thank you," he said softly as he helped her into the buggy. "It means a lot to me that you're not looking down at her."

When he got into the buggy, she leaned toward him, whispering, "If you had courted me in the usual way, I have a feeling I wouldn't have been a virgin on our wedding night. How can I say anything against her when I could have been the same?"

He grinned. "I guess that might be true..."

"Where are her parents?" she asked. "I would think they'd sit with her at church."

"No, they moved away shortly after she started showing. Her father was an associate of my father. He worked for Father in the bank, and they were quite close. He was thrilled to see her engaged to one of us, but when Jesse died, and she was pregnant, well that was all he cared about. They moved back east."

"That's terrible! Didn't they ask her to go? They could have passed her off as a widow..."

"I suggested that to him, but he said he couldn't stand the sight of her after she'd shamed him the way she had. So she stayed here, and I helped as I could."

"Were you with her on Wednesday night after I was so awful to you?" Florence asked.

He shrugged. "I went to her for a few minutes. I never stay more than ten in her home so there won't be more talk. I told her what had happened, and that she should stay away from you because I thought you'd treat her as everyone else did. I'm so glad to be wrong."

"I guess we were both wrong about different things, weren't we?"

He put his arm around her and kissed her atop her head. He'd married the right woman, and there was no doubt about it.

Chapter Nine

Just before noon on Monday, Kate arrived with Jesse and a book of dress designs. "Are we too early?" she asked.

Florence shook her head with a grin on her face. "Not at all."

"What's so funny?" Kate asked.

"Jake has this theory that people wait outside until the exact minute they're supposed to be somewhere before they knock. We experienced it, and then we went five minutes early to someone's house, and they commented on how early we were."

Kate smiled. "Jesse and I did silly things like that as well."

"I'm sure you miss him terribly. I know Jake does."

Kate's eyes misted. "I do. And I wish Jesse could know his father, but at least he has his Uncle Jake, who looks just like his papa did."

"You have my deepest sympathies. And I will help with anything I can in any way I can."

"I've gotten that impression. Thank you. And I'm sorry for throwing a bag of candy at you."

Florence smiled. "It's already forgotten."

The two women went into the dining room where Mrs. Andrews was putting food on the table. "It's so good to see you!" Kate said, hugging the older woman.

"I wish you'd come more often," Mrs. Andrews said. "I'll feed the boy in the kitchen." She looked down at Jesse and lifted him into her arms. "Do you want to eat in the kitchen with me like your daddy used to do?"

Jesse nodded emphatically, and the two disappeared into the kitchen.

Florence took Jake's usual spot at the head of the table and noticed that Kate's spot was set right beside her. No yelling down the table. Just the way she preferred things.

As they ate, Florence mentioned what she was looking for in dresses. "I never realized just how much better my mother was at dressing me than I am. I do hope you'll have opinions to share on what would look good and what wouldn't."

"I seem to have a good eye. I planned to make dresses when my parents left, but no one would hire me for anything but shirts. I'm excited to have someone to wear the dresses I've designed."

"I'll do more than that. Anytime I'm complimented on one of them, I'll make sure the person knows I got it from you and that you're the best seamstress around."

Kate frowned. "Now, you can't praise me for my work unless you like it."

"All right. I can agree to that. I'm excited to look through your designs. Have you been trained in any way?" Florence asked.

Kate shook her head. "I went to finishing school back east, and I was allowed to learn basic sewing. I talked my mother into buying me a machine, so I could make my own clothes, but nothing beyond that. I have the sewing machine, and I use it for everything I make, so everything is quick."

"But you mostly taught yourself all this?" Florence shook her head. "For someone who was raised the same way I was, that's amazing. I can arrange flowers, and I'm more than capable of planning a party. Beyond that, I have no real skills in life. I don't know what I'd do in your position."

Kate shrugged. "You're too smart to be in my position."

Florence frowned. "I don't think so. If I was engaged to Jake, I have a feeling we would have anticipated our vows. The difference would be whether or not Jake died. I can easily see myself as a young mother trying to raise a child on my own. I'm thankful it didn't turn out that way, but I certainly don't think less of you for it."

Kate tilted her head to one side, studying Florence. "We're going to be friends, aren't we?"

"I hope so!" Florence said. Kate was just the type of person she wanted to be friends with.

"I'm glad. I'll give you my friend discount."

"You will not! I'm paying full price for whatever you make for me."

"But you'll be my model, showing off my styles. I can't charge you full price when you do that."

"Of course, you can. Jake wouldn't have it any other way, and neither would I."

"I don't know what I would have done without Jake's friendship over the last few years. He's been a rock."

"He's a good man through and through," Florence said.

After they'd finished their lunch, Mrs. Andrews said she would see to little Jesse and make sure he got his nap, so the women went into the blue parlor to look at dresses. Kate had brought many different fabric swatches as well to help make things easier.

"My favorite dress is long-sleeved, full-skirted, and ice blue. The blue stands out on me. I think I want more dresses in that color."

Kate nodded, making a note. "Do we want to make it your signature color? So everything I make is that color, and people can pick you out of a crowd based on what you're wearing?"

Florence smiled. "I do like that idea. Maybe not all dresses but most?"

"That sounds good. And I'm designing evening gowns or day dresses?"

"Both," Florence said, knowing Kate needed the money far more than she herself needed dresses. "Perhaps all the evening gowns should be in that ice blue, but we can have a variety of colors for my day dresses."

Kate nodded, making a quick note. "I think that's a wonderful idea."

Together, the two women—the unlikeliest of friends—sat and created a wardrobe. At the end of Kate's book there were some items of lingerie, and even though it was embarrassing to discuss with a friend, she ordered several items in silk. She loved the feel of silk on her skin, and Jake seemed to expect it.

The final bill was more money than Florence had imagined, but she knew Jake wouldn't complain if it was to help Kate. "Let me pay you half now, so you can buy the fabric."

Kate looked relieved. "Thank you for thinking of that. I was going to have to buy enough for only two dresses and then bring them to you and use that money for the next ones."

"No need for that. I'll be right back."

Florence hurried up the stairs and found the money she'd hidden in all the trunks and on her person before heading west. She couldn't think of a better use of the emergency fund her parents had given her than helping a friend.

When she reached the blue parlor again, she carefully counted out the money to Kate. "Is that enough to buy what you need to buy?"

Kate nodded. "And enough for Jesse and I to live on as I finish these dresses. May I bringing you two or three pieces at a time, so I can make certain my sewing is up to your standards?"

"I'd like that a lot," Florence said, all at once excited to get the new clothes. For so long, shopping had been something she dreaded, due to the way her mother had forced it upon her. Now, she had made the choices with a trusted friend, and she would be wearing styles no one else had even seen.

"I have one more dress that I have in mind for you, but it's not in the book. May I create something for you and it be a surprise?" Kate asked, looking excited at the prospect.

"I would love that. Thank you so much." Florence would have to order another armoire for all the clothes she was having Kate make, but she knew she'd look her best and the money would be very helpful to Kate and Jesse.

"All right then. Let's get your measurements, and then we'll see what Mrs. Andrews has done with my baby."

Florence laughed. "Treated him like a king is what she's done."

"Oh, I know. He'll act spoiled for days." Kate didn't mind that her son was getting spoiled. "She's the closest thing he has to a grandmother."

"I wish your parents had accepted him."

Kate shrugged. "I made a mistake, and I'm paying for it. But I wouldn't change it for the world because I have Jesse."

Later that afternoon, Florence couldn't quit thinking about what Kate had said. She wouldn't go back and change her actions because she wouldn't have Jesse. Florence knew she wouldn't change what had happened between Arthur and herself because she wouldn't have Jake.

When she'd agreed to marry a stranger, she'd thought she was settling for second best, but she knew now it had been meant to happen this way. Jake was not second to anyone.

ON WEDNESDAY EVENING, she and Jake headed out to the Wilson residence, and Florence was excited to see the kindest of Jake female friends she'd met. As they drove, she asked him what had happened the previous year.

"Mrs. Wilson told me that they almost lost their home last year, but that you'd prevented that from happening."

Jake shrugged. "I'm a banker. I do what I can."

"So you helped them in your position as bank president?" she asked.

He sighed. "I guess I need to tell you the whole story, but you cannot tell anyone else. Please."

"What happened?"

"They lost a large portion of their herd to blizzards two winters ago, and they didn't have enough cattle left to go to sale. The bank couldn't loan them money because they weren't an acceptable risk, so I loaned them money personally because I know them and believe in them. Mr. Wilson will pay me back next month, and he has the herd to do it now. It was the right thing to do."

"And you always do the right thing," Florence said softly. "I truly admire you."

"Oh, stop that!" he said. "I don't want to be admired."

"I'll do my best," she said.

When they got to the Wilson's home, they were invited in immediately. Mrs. Wilson invited her into the kitchen to chat while she finished the last of the meal. Florence was a little surprised they didn't have a housekeeper cooking for them.

"I can see the question on your face," Mrs. Wilson said. "I had to let my housekeeper go, and we tightened our belts after our money troubles. She's staying with her daughter for a while, and after we sell off our steers next month, she'll be coming back. I wasn't raised as you were. I learned to cook and clean, and I was the one who kept our house until about ten years ago. It wasn't a problem for me to do it all again."

"It must be frightening to know that a bad winter can completely change your life."

Mrs. Wilson nodded. "Yes, it is at times. We're very thankful to Jake for what he did for us. Mr. Wilson went to the bank first, of course, but the loan officer told us that his hands were tied. When Jake saw we'd been denied, he drove out here to talk to us about what he could do. He didn't even charge us interest. Anytime I hear anyone say anything against Jake, I stand up for him because he's a *good* man. There aren't enough of those around."

"Thank you for being the voice of reason with all the gossiping in this town. You'd think Kate was the first person to ever have a child out of wedlock."

"I've heard rumors you've made friends with Kate, and I have to say I'm impressed. I'm not sure I could do the same."

"It was easy," Florence said. "She's going to make me some gowns, and I'm excited to see them."

Mrs. Wilson smiled. "I really like you, Mrs. Weatherby."

"Won't you call me Florence?"

"Only if you call me Louise."

"Happily," Florence said. "Now what can I do to help?"

Together they carried the food into the dining room and placed it on the table. While Louise went to fetch the men, Florence rearranged the flowers in the vase on the table, making them look as if they had been professionally done.

As they all sat down to eat, Mr. Wilson said a prayer over the meal. The discussion they shared felt like the first real conversation she'd had with another woman since she'd arrived in Wyoming. It was nice to finally find a friend, but she couldn't help but wonder how Louise had been before she'd needed Jake's money.

Finally, she decided it didn't matter at all. If Louise had been one of the negative women, she'd learned her lesson and was much kinder now.

On the way home, Florence couldn't stop smiling. "I'm glad to finally have two friends here. I didn't think I'd ever be able to make friends with any of the women who run in our circle."

"Why is that?" he asked.

"Because they all talk about you. Only Louise has anything nice to say. I'm sick of listening to all the gossip about you as if you're a terrible person."

"I'm glad you're on my side," he said after a while. "When you weren't, you were a bit scary."

She laughed. "You should have seen me when Arthur told me he'd stepped out on me and married someone else."

He glanced at her and then back at the horses. "Why?"

"I kicked him two or three times and slapped his face and hit him with our guest list for the wedding, though that didn't hurt him. I was furious."

He shook his head. "I'd have had to send you home after all that!"

"This is home," she told him, resting her head on his shoulder. "Anywhere you are is my home."

"And if I decide to move into a log cabin in the mountains?"

"I'll follow you. It may take me a little while to learn to cook, but I'd dedicate myself to learning as quickly as I could."

He laughed. "I won't do that because I'm afraid of what I'd have to eat."

She giggled. "It would not be pretty. I always told my mother I wanted to learn to cook just in case I ever needed to, but she always refused."

"I promise, if I decide to move somewhere with no housekeeper, I'll ensure you get cooking lessons first. See? I'm thinking about our future."

"You always do!"

"Oh, I forgot to mention to you. I donated a few new beds to the local hospital, and they're doing a fundraiser on Friday night of next week, and I'll be honored there. I asked them not to honor me, and they said it was necessary, so we're having a night out."

"All right. I can help with party planning if there's room for me. I need to start getting involved in local charities anyway. I worked in our orphanage in Massachusetts."

"No need," he said. "I want you to ease into society slowly. I never know what someone is going to say about me."

Chapter Ten

There were three more dinner parties before the big event at the hospital, and Florence was barraged by gossip about her husband at each one. Trying to shut the women down turned out to be a great deal more difficult than she'd imagined it would be.

For the hospital fundraiser, Florence wore her first evening gown created by Kate. When she looked in the mirror in her room, she was thrilled by the way the skirt flared out when she spun. This was the first dance she would be attending after moving to Cheyenne, and she looked forward to every minute of it.

This time there would be no gossip about Jake because he was being honored at this event. No one would dare talk about him at an event that he was the guest of honor for.

When they arrived, Florence realized she knew almost everyone there, which was a bit of a surprise. Surely, she hadn't met everyone in town yet.

Jake and Florence walked to the table where they were collecting things to auction off to help with the hospital. They wanted to add another wing to the building so there would be room for whoever needed it. At the moment, they often had to turn patients away because there was simply not enough room.

Florence carried with her a coupon for a free evening gown from Kate. She would pay Kate for the work and the fabric, but someone else would have to see just how wonderful Kate's work was.

Jake walked away to talk to a group of men, and Florence walked to a group of women, all of whom she'd met. To her dismay, it didn't seem that the fact Jake was being honored was stemming any of the gossip.

"I can't believe they're honoring Jacob Weatherby," one woman said, and for a moment, Florence struggled to remember her name, but then realized she had no desire to know who it was.

"I know. I feel so sorry for his wife. She didn't know what she was getting into when she married him."

Florence bit her lip and smiled sweetly as she joined the others. "There's no reason to feel sorry for me. I'm quite happy in my marriage."

The woman who had spoken first flushed, and Florence realized it was Mrs. Whitaker. "Your dress is pretty," Mrs. Whitaker said.

"Thank you so much. Kate made it for me. She's a genius when it comes to fabric and designs. I brought a coupon for one of her evening gowns, so if you like it, you should bid on it."

"I don't think I'll be doing that. You may be able to be friends with your husband's former mistress, but the rest of us will never go to her for our gowns, will we, ladies?"

The women all nodded, leaving Florence feeling as if these women should all be kicked out of the party. "She's making me an entire new wardrobe," Florence said as if the other woman hadn't said anything. "I'm so happy with this one, I just had to wear it tonight."

When no one responded to that, Florence brought up the weather. "Do you think winter will set in soon?" she asked.

"It usually is upon us before the end of October," one of the women responded.

"And it's already the end of September. Surely, we have more than a month before snow flies."

"Not usually," Mrs. Whitaker said.

Florence noticed another circle of women and decided to join them. Hopefully they had the manners to keep them from being rude about Jake. "If you'll all excuse me," she said as she made a beeline for the other group.

She heard the women just before reaching them. "Jacob Weatherby thinks he's going to buy his way into the good graces of this community. I for one am sick of him acting as if he's never done a thing wrong when we all know he has."

Florence closed her eyes and counted to ten, trying to calm her temper, but this time, it didn't want to be calmed. So she raised her voice, and said what needed to be said. "All of the women in this town act as though my husband is the worst kind of scoundrel. He's the man who donated beds to this hospital. He's the man who takes care of people in this town when they run into trouble financially.

"I know all of you consider yourselves good Christian women. Do any of you pay attention to the fact that every sin is the same in God's eyes? As all of you stand here gossiping you are just as guilty of sin as the man I love, though all of you consider him beneath you. None of you have one bit of evidence to share that would make me believe my husband is a wrongdoer, yet I stand here and have heard each of you gossip about a man who has done nothing but help this community!"

Florence shook her head. "Have none of you read the scripture at Matthew 7:3-5? 'And why thou beholdest thou the mote that is in thy brother's eye, but considerest not the beam that is in thine own eye? Or how wilt thou say to thy brother, Let me pull out the mote out of thing eye; and behold, a beam is in thine own eye? Thou hypocrite, first cast out the beam out of thine own eye; and then shalt thou see clearly to cast out the mote out of thy brother's eye.'"

Many of the women gasped, but Florence ignored them and continued. "I know my sin. It's anger. And it's anger with each of you for saying things about the man I love that should never be said. Not by Christian women anyway. I will now say, we will no longer accept invitations from anyone who gossips about my husband. And we will no longer bestow invitations to people who gossip about Jacob. If you have gossiped, and I know about it, then you'll go on a list of people we will not be socializing with. You may submit a written apology if you wish to come off my list."

Florence was shaking when she turned around to head to the door. But instead of a path being opened for her, her husband stood in front of her, having obviously heard the whole thing. "I'm sorry, Jake, but I can't stay here another minute. I think I need to cool off for a short while."

Jake offered her his arm and escorted her to the door and outside. "I'm so sorry!" she said. "I know you didn't want me to do that, but I just couldn't restrain myself."

He grinned for a moment, but then his grin turned into a rumble as he laughed from deep within his belly. "I didn't hear what led up to what you said, but I certainly heard what you said. You are a true gem." He leaned down and pressed his lips to hers, not caring who was watching. "Thank you for defending me." Gathering her close he held her as she stopped shaking. "I can't leave yet. I need to go and receive my letter of thanks."

"If I can have just five more minutes to breathe, I think I can go back in with you. The women in this town deserve to be horsewhipped. I cannot believe how disrespectful they are to you!"

He leaned down and kissed her again. "I don't care what any of them think about me or say behind my back. I only care what you think and say, and if that's an example of what you say behind my back, I can only say thank you."

She took another deep breath. "You don't care that I gave all of them an ultimatum?"

"Did they deserve it?" he asked.

Florence nodded emphatically. "I thought tonight no one would gossip about you because you were the guest of honor. But they still do. I don't understand how people can be so mean and petty."

"I don't either, but it doesn't matter anymore. As long as you believe in me so strongly, I can get through this."

"Does that mean you trust me again?" she asked.

"After that, how could I not?" Jake was still grinning at her as if she had done something wondrous.

"Let's go back in. Now they'll all be talking about me, but I don't even care. As long as they don't let your name touch their lips."

Inside again, Florence was well aware of how everyone's eyes followed her. She worried she may have gone a bit too far, but the more she thought about it, the more she wished she'd said more. She should have told them all they weren't good enough to have Jake's name pass her lips.

Quickly, there was a line of men, apologizing for their wives' behavior. Mr. Whitaker was at the front of the line. "I'm so sorry my wife has gossiped about you. At first, she talked to me about it but when I told her not marrying a woman carrying your child was out of character for you, she started talking to the other women instead."

Jake nodded. "I understand. I'll be waiting for your wife's letter of apology."

As Florence watched, he said the same thing to each of the men. He wasn't mean about it. He just kept saying he'd wait for the letter of apology that should be forthcoming. She couldn't believe he was going to hold the women to what she'd said.

Of course, she didn't care if they never socialized again. She had two friends, and that was enough for her. Why would she want to be friends with people who said bad things about her husband anyway?

When the letter of thanks was presented to Jake, Florence stood at his side, making eye contact with as many of the women as she could. She couldn't call them ladies because they certainly didn't act like they were anything but wretched gutter tramps.

When the first dance was announced, Jake took her into his arms and spun her about the dancefloor as if they were in a grand ballroom. Florence found she didn't care where she was as long as she was in Jake's arms.

When it came time to bid for the different items, Florence found that her donation went for much more than she'd expected. Perhaps the women had listened to her and learned something.

Of course, she was one of the youngest of the women there, and she was fairly certain her words had only touched the men who would no longer tolerate their wives gossip of a good man, who was a true friend to all of them.

After the bidding, during which Florence bought a few of the items there, one a painting that she thought would look wonderful in the blue parlor, Jake told her it was time for them to leave.

For once, she didn't mind being the first couple who left. She would be happy if she didn't have to look at anyone of those women again, but she knew it couldn't work out that way.

After they'd arrived at home, Jake led her upstairs. "Do you really love me? Or was that just something you said in the heat of the moment?"

"Of course, I love you. You're the best man I have ever met, and you make my knees weak."

"How do I do that?" he asked, moving toward her.

"How do you think?"

He chuckled. "I love you too, Florence. I knew I was in love with you from the first moment I saw you, and I thought our marriage would be all sunshine and roses. I only felt the thorns for a couple of days, but I haven't told you how very much I care because of those two days."

"I can understand that very well," she said. "I made a mess of things very early on, and I wish I could have trusted you the way I trust you now."

LETTERS OF APOLOGY started pouring in the following morning. Many had small gifts attached to them such as a basket of fruit or some rather delicious cookies. And to the last letter, each woman had written two letters. One to apologize to Jake and another to apologize to Florence for making her first weeks in Cheyenne miserable.

Florence laughed as she told Jake of everyone assuming her first weeks there were miserable. "I guess it's a good thing they couldn't see us when we were together privately. My first weeks here were far from miserable. They were spent with you."

He smiled, reached for her, and groaned when there was yet another knock on the door. Going to open it, he found Kate and Jesse standing there, and invited them in. "She's in the blue parlor."

Kate found Florence in the parlor and hugged her. "I have orders for six more dresses."

"That's wonderful! Take a break from doing mine and get theirs done immediately. That will keep them coming back to you."

"I don't know how to thank you."

"Forgive me for how I acted when I first arrived? I need nothing more."

"I forgave you long ago," Kate said, shaking her head. "I'm so excited!"

"You earned those new customers. I wore that first gown last night for the hospital benefit, and I received a compliment on it and ensured everyone knew you'd made it."

"Thank you!"

Jake walked in then with little Jesse on his shoulders. "He looks so much like you," Florence observed.

"My brother and I were identical twins. He looks like his father, but at the same time, he looks like me. If that makes any kind of sense at all."

"I suppose it does." Florence shook her head, enjoying looking at them together. She hoped she would have a boy just as handsome as Jesse.

"Well, I had to come and thank you," Kate said. "I'm glad you came here and married Jake. You are exactly what he needed."

Florence smiled. "If only I could control my temper."

Kate laughed. "I did hear some things about what you said last night..."

Jake grinned. "I couldn't have been prouder of her. And we've gotten letters of apology from every woman who was there last night and several more. I think they're all afraid of Florence now."

"Good!" Kate said. "I know I'll still be gossiped about, but I've gotten used to that."

"I could make another announcement at the next party we attend..." Florence said, grinning.

"As long as they buy gowns from me, I don't care what they say behind my back!"

Epilogue

Jake stood in front of the window in their bedroom, holding his twin daughters. They were identical, just as he and his brother had been. "I hope you both find a man who completes you," he said softly. "Your mama is the best thing that ever happened to me, and I want you to both say that about your husbands one day."

He glanced over his shoulder to where Florence was sleeping. "She's tired. You two wore her out coming into this world. I hope you both have the same amount of passion for the people you love your mama does. She's an amazing lady."

The babies were sleeping in his arms, and had no response, but that was all right, because he hadn't expected one.